P9-COP-353

Sex with Spirit

An Illustrated Guide to Techniques and Traditions

Michelle Pauli

Red Wheel
Boston, MA / York Beach, ME

First published in the USA in 2002 by
Red Wheel/Weiser, LLC
York Beach, ME

With editorial offices at:
368 Congress Street
Boston, MA 02210
www.redwheelweiser.com

08 07 06 05 04 03 02
7 6 5 4 3 2 1

Editor: Geoffrey Chesler
Design: Axis Design Editions Ltd

ISBN 1–59003–021–4

Printed and bound in France by ***Partenaires-Livres***® (J.L. 04/02)

The paper in this publication meets the minimum requirements of the American National Standard for Information Sciences—Permanence of Paper for Printed Library Materials Z39.48–1992 (R1997).

Contents

INTRODUCTION

The Alchemy of Sex

The only transformer
and alchemist
That turns everything
into gold is love.

ANAÏS NIN

To discover the mysteries of sacred sex is to embark upon a journey of joy. The ancient path of ecstatic sexuality, leading to a state of enlightenment and bliss, has long been traveled by followers in many different spiritual traditions. Each tradition has developed distinctive ways to cultivate and harness the potency of sexual energy, affirming the vital connection of body, mind, and spirit.

Sacred sex harmonizes the dual energies within each of us—whether we call them God and Goddess, Yin and Yang, or darkness and light—using passion and intimacy to combine and direct those forces both within and between ourselves. Through this process we break through the limitations of the personal self and experience a sense of oneness with creation. Infusing our sexual relationships with spirituality, we take our pleasure to a new dimension—transforming our sexual drive into spiritual energy, transcending the physical body, and entering a state of heightened consciousness.

Sex with Spirit introduces the beliefs and reveals the lovemaking secrets of a number of sexual-spiritual traditions, including Tantra, Taoism, Wicca, and Sex Magick. You may be inspired to investigate a particular path further, or to weave the practices into your own belief system, or simply to expand and clarify your thoughts. You can work straight through the book as a guide, from the preparation of body and mind through to advanced postures and techniques, or you can pick and choose interesting ideas and alternative approaches. These are offered as suggestions, to be adapted and altered as you feel comfortable, or used as a starting point for further exploration.

Many of the exercises in the book can be practiced on your own. Getting to know your own body and your sexual responses profoundly influences your sexual and emotional confidence. Some energy-raising and moving exercises are best practiced without a partner, and there is a long tradition in Buddhist Tantra and in Sex Magickal work of solo cultivation. Understanding, expressing, and fulfilling your own sexuality is a process that is inherently life-affirming, and it forms a solid base from which to explore heightened sexual bliss with future lovers.

Sacred sex is a path of love and acceptance that is open to everybody, whether you are straight or gay, single or in a long-term relationship. The focus on harmonizing male and female energies does not confine it exclusively to heterosexual couples. We all contain both polarities of energy, and gay singles or couples can play with these energies just as effectively as heterosexuals. Where exercises refer specifically to male and female partners they can, in almost all cases, be adapted for same-sex couples.

For those who are in a long-term relationship, an interest in sacred sex may arise from a feeling that their relationship has started to become a little flat, and has lost its initial spark and excitement. Spiritualizing your sex life can help you to rekindle that spark, and take it to new heights of passion and ecstasy. In re-visioning your relationship as a meeting of divine energies, in which you celebrate each other with devotion, you can radically change the way you view and treat your lover, which has beneficial effects on every part of your daily lives together.

Incorporating sacred sex into your love life will take time and commitment. The idea of "scheduling" sexual intimacy in advance may seem a little cold and unromantic, but an expression of commitment is a necessary precondition for spiritual advancement. Training the mind, working on the body, and practicing together create the conditions for blissful liberation. Knowing that you have set aside a specific time for a session of ritual lovemaking can spice up the rest of your day as well.

Making love with purposeful consciousness transforms a sexual relationship into a gateway to the divine, and reconnects us to our spiritual origins. The sexual act is only the start of the journey. As we feel the energy of life, the energy of creation, coursing within ourselves during sexual union, we are offered an insight into the interconnectedness of all things. Sacred sexuality leads us to realize that we were sacred all along.

Enjoy the journey!

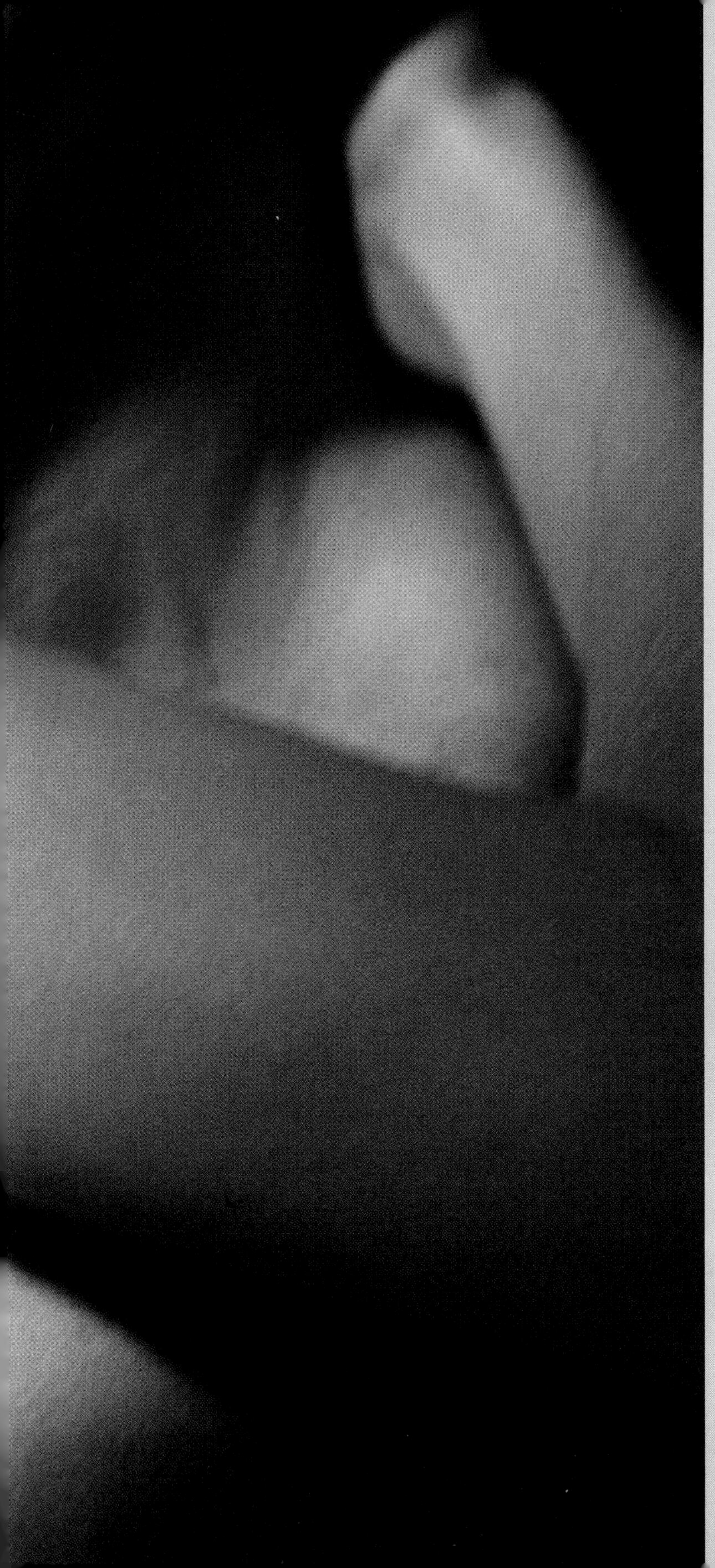

CHAPTER 1

Sex and Spirituality

In most mainstream religious traditions, sex has long been regarded as an obstacle to spiritual progress, something to be overcome and transcended. Earthly desires are seen as sinful, and sexual restraint—even celibacy—is thought by many to hold the key to spiritual knowledge and experience. However, there are two Eastern paths with a refreshingly different perspective. Tantra and Taoism both take the approach that one should not only not reject the body and its desires, but actually embrace them on the road to enlightenment. They share the view that sexual intercourse can be a sacrament and a means of spiritual transformation.

These ideas can also be found in the West. The pre-Christian pagan traditions of Europe celebrate and honor sexuality, regarding the act of love as a way of worshipping the Great Goddess and her consort; and the present-day practice of Sex Magick recognizes and harnesses the natural power of sexual energy in ritual.

Tantra

Love, enjoyed by the ignorant,
Becomes bondage.
That very same love,
tasted by one with understanding,
Brings liberation.

Enjoy all the pleasures of love fearlessly,
For the sake of liberation.

CITTAVISUDDHIPRAKARANA

The ancient cult of Tantra originated in India's earliest tribal societies, long predating the first Tantric texts, which were probably written in the sixth century CE. The Sanskrit word *tantra* is related to the concept of weaving and expansion—it derives from *tan*, meaning to expand, spin out, and weave. We weave the disparate strands of our nature into a unified whole, and so grow and expand into joy. Tantra can also refer to those teachings in the sacred Hindu texts that are generally presented in the form of a dialog between the god Shiva and his consort Shakti, whose joyful coupling creates and sustains the universe.

Unlike Western religion that polarizes the sacred and the profane, Tantra regards our physical senses as vehicles of liberation and enlightenment. Its goal is the reintegration of body and mind. It sees the macrocosm—the realms of heaven and spirit—reflected in, and accessible through, the microcosm of the Earth and the human body.

Tantra is a spiritual science that works with action, in which every aspect of worldly existence is approached as an act of worship. Enlightenment can be found in all forms of activity, including sexual intimacy, and the practitioner's aim is to transform the everyday into the divine. In Tantra all the senses are harnessed, and the experience of ecstasy is sought as a spiritual tool. Desire is mastered, not through the flight from pleasure, but by total immersion in it.

Tantra offers a radical shortcut to spiritual illumination, holding that it can be attained in a single lifetime by cutting directly through ordinary awareness and conventional thought patterns. The everyday world of illusion coexists with the eternal, and enlightenment is achieved by realizing that each level of reality contains, and interlaces with, the greater transcendent whole.

Right Shiva and Shakti in her incarnation as the beautiful goddess Parvati. This eleventh-century erotic carving is from the great Hindu temple complex in Khajuraho, Madhya Pradesh, India.

Tantra's non-hierarchical, non-judgmental, and all-accepting approach toward experience was a challenge to both Hindu and Buddhist cultures. The view that enlightenment could be achieved by all men and women, regardless of their backgrounds, was revolutionary in caste-bound India. Many of its followers came from the lower castes, and much of its practice was specifically designed to break down barriers and taboos. Buddhist Tantra arose outside of the powerful Buddhist monasteries, in the eighth to twelfth centuries CE, as a protest movement, initially championed by laypeople with the aim of creating a more accessible and inclusive religious system.

Many of Tantra's magical rites were deliberately rebellious and non-conformist, designed to shock in order to break through prejudices and so leave the adept open to the experience of Oneness. While some Tantric methods of transforming energy to aid spiritual evolution—such as visualization, sitting meditation, and breathing—could be performed entirely as an internal practice, the "left-hand path" embraced sexuality as a gateway to transformation and liberation. It allowed men and women to pursue enlightenment together through a series of ritualized expressions of intimacy that would transform the energy of their physical passion into spiritual ecstasy.

The central Tantric ceremony, known as the Five Ms, highlights its convention-defying nature. This takes place at night, and is attended by a number of couples who ritually enjoy the five pleasures ordinarily forbidden to high-caste Hindus—*madya* (wine), *matsya* (fish), *mamsa* (meat), followed by *mudra* (parched grain), and culminating in *maithuna* (sexual intercourse).

Tantra, particularly the Tibetan Buddhist schools, uses the rapture of sexual union as a basis for meditation. By maintaining a clear realization of emptiness in the midst of passion, it becomes possible to turn that passion into supreme bliss. Sexual arousal is used ritually, as a sacrament, to weave together the inner and outer realities.

Buddhist and Hindu Tantra shared an emphasis on feminine, goddess power, and on women as embodiments of female divinity. The universe was considered to be generated by the primeval female energy of Shakti, and men were required to honor and worship their female partners. Female Buddhas started to appear in religious iconography for the first time, along with symbolic images of Buddhist deities coupling in sacred union.

In Hindu Tantra the sacred union of opposites is epitomized by the cosmic dance of Shakti and Shiva. When they embrace, love ripples through the universe.

Shakti is the creative force behind all existence, whom all women embody. She is depicted by a range of deities who represent her various qualities, such as Parvati, goddess of beauty, Mohini the temptress, and Kali the destroyer.

Shiva is the male energy of pure consciousness who needs Shakti to give him form, just as she needs him to give her consciousness. In this way they act as complementary forces, depending upon each other in order to be whole. Their union is the union of energy and consciousness, which creates bliss, and the entire physical and transcendental world is continuously created by their interplay. Men also have the feminine principle within them, in the form of Kundalini energy—the individual's latent store of energy, visualized as a coiled snake at the base of the spine. Tantrics seek to awaken Kundalini energy and direct it upward to unite with Shiva energy in the crown of the head. To experience the dynamic balance of consciousness and energy, all individuals must achieve an inner marriage of their masculine and feminine natures.

Tantric couples worship each other as embodiments of the divine male and female principles. They make love as Shakti and Shiva, and use spiritual, psychological, and physical lovemaking techniques to heighten and transform their sexual energy into the bliss of liberation.

Neo-Tantra

Tantra has always adapted itself to suit its time and place, and this is no less true of its migration to the West in the 1960s. The form that developed there dispenses with many of the culturally specific beliefs and rituals of traditional Hindu and Buddhist Tantra, and as such it is more properly known as "Neo-Tantra." It found a ready audience in the 'sixties generation: the sexual revolution, overseas travel, an interest in mysticism and all things Eastern, and minds opened by psychedelic drugs, had all prepared the ground for spiritual sexuality.

In the 1970s the Indian guru Osho (formerly Bhagwan Shree Rajneesh) further popularized Tantric sexuality as a viable path for Westerners with a special fusion of Tantra and psychotherapy that bridged the cultural divide.

Elements from psychotherapy also feature in many Neo-Tantra programs taught today. These workshops and seminars tend to concentrate on the quality of the relationship, and apply Tantric techniques, removed from the original framework of Hindu culture and religion, as a way of developing and enhancing a couple's intimacy. In traditional Tantra, by contrast, intimacy is achieved in sexual union through the creation of a shared visionary universe, and the goal of the relationship is enlightenment.

Taoism

The Tao produced One;
One produced Two;
Two produced Three;
Three produced All things.

TAO TE CHING

Taoism is the joyful Chinese spiritual tradition that extols the "way of nature"—the Chinese word *tao* means "way." The true origins of Taoism are lost in the mists of time; legend ascribes it to the mythical founder of all Chinese civilization, the Yellow Emperor, Huang Ti. However, two books written in around the fourth century BCE, the *Chuang-Tz'u* and the *Lao-Tz'u* (or *Tao Te Ching*), are the foundational texts to which all later schools refer. Of the two texts, it is the *Tao Te Ching* that most fully encapsulates Taoist philosophy.

The Tao is conceived of as the universal creative principle underlying all forms, substances, beings, and changes. It is seen in the harmonious interplay of the negative (*yin*) and positive (*yang*) energies that permeate the cosmos, and it represents the conjunction of all opposites. The Tao dynamically underlies all creative life, and is the source of all phenomena. It is the all-pervasive state of being, on which humans ought to model themselves if they are to realize their potential and progress spiritually.

Taoists seek to live harmoniously with the Tao. They do this in part through practicing the principle of *wu wei*, "not acting." This means not inaction, but ceasing to act through the ego, or "acting in harmony with nature." By releasing themselves from attachments, they create an inner space, enabling the Tao to enter them. Only action flowing from this still center is in harmony with the Way.

The Tao can be thought of as energy, movement, and constant change, in which balanced and harmonious opposites continually unite and metamorphose into each other—these opposites are represented by Yin and Yang. The vital energy that flows between the two is called *chi*.

The dynamic tension between Yin and Yang results in an endless process of creation and destruction, driven by change, always entailing the production, reproduction, and transformation of energy. Yin and Yang are mutually interdependent, constantly interactive, and potentially interchangeable forces. Their ceaseless state of flux means that the primary attribute of the Tao is constant change.

Yin symbolizes darkness, passivity, yielding, and softness. It moves downward and inward and is represented by woman, water, and earth. Yang symbolizes light, activity, resistance, hardness, and expansion. It moves upward and outward and is represented by man, fire, and heaven. While Yin is the feminine power and Yang the masculine, by their very cyclical nature there can be no pure Yin or pure Yang. All phenomena have these two aspects to them. Each individual is an expression of both masculine and feminine energies, while within the human race women embody Yin principles and men represent Yang.

Below This cheery erotic scene is imbued with the spirit of Tao. It is one of a series of Chinese prints depicting the lives and legendary skills of Mongol horsemen. Tao-kung period, c. 1850.

The harmonious balancing of the forces of Yin and Yang is the principle underlying all Taoist disciplines, including herbal medicine, diet, exercises, and breathing techniques. Because the Taoists saw physical, psychological, and spiritual well-being as inseparable, they developed a practical and coherent system of cultivating well-being.

As part of their empirical search for long life and spiritual advancement, the Taoist masters investigated the healing power of lovemaking. This emphasis on health represents a major difference between Taoism and Tantra—in Taoism lovemaking is regarded as a natural science within medicine, to be studied and understood, rather than as a purely religious path.

In direct contrast to the taboo-ridden attitudes of the Judeo-Christian traditions, the Taoists viewed sexual activity as vital and energizing, bringing Yin and Yang forces together in an exchange of positive and negative energies. Sexual union was regarded as the earthly manifestation of the great cosmic dance, and part of the natural order of things—a key to the acquisition of health, longevity, and, ultimately, spiritual perfection.

Some Taoists compiled manuals of sexual technique, also known as "pillow books." These offered advice on Taoist lovemaking techniques, in the form of dialogs between sages and (archetypal) initiatory women. According to Chinese legend, the Yellow Emperor was introduced to sexual life by a triad of sexual initiators—Su-nu (the foremost of these), the Plain Girl; Hsuan-nu, the Dark Girl; and Tsa'ai-nu, the Elected Girl. Their dialogs with the Emperor can be found in the classic Chinese erotic texts, the *Sexual Handbook of the Dark Girl*, the *Classic of the Secret Methods of the Plain Girl*, and the *Sexual Recipes of the Plain Girl*.

Traditionally, these early sex manuals were used by newly married couples, and could even form part of the bride's trousseau. Their use is beautifully shown in a poem by Cheng Heng (78–139 CE):

I have swept clean the pillow and bedmat,
And have fitted the burner with rare incense.
Let us now lock the double door with the golden lock,
And light the lamp to fill our room with brilliance.
I shed my robes and remove my paint and powder,
And roll out the picture scroll by the pillow.
The Plain Girl I shall take as my instructress,
So that we may practice all the variegated postures,
Those that an ordinary husband has but rarely seen,
Such as taught by Tien-Lo to the Yellow Emperor.

Although written in poetic language, the "pillow books" contain practical guidelines and explicit instruction on a variety of different aspects of lovemaking, from foreplay and sexual positions to special thrusting techniques. They place as much emphasis on female as on male satisfaction, offering frank advice on arousing a woman and understanding her sexual needs. In answer to the question, "How do I know when a woman feels the joys of sex?" the Yellow Emperor is offered step-by-step instructions on how to spot both the voluntary and the involuntary responses of an aroused woman, and how to navigate his way through them so as to provide the greatest pleasure.

The female initiators did not confine themselves to revealing how to tell when a woman is prepared for sex. The Dark Girl also set out the signs by which a man can understand if he is properly prepared for intercourse. His "jade stalk" must pass through four stages of attainment—elongation, swelling, hardness, and heat. Once these stages have been reached, his muscles and bones are harmonized with his energy and spirit, and he is in a suitably balanced state to enjoy and reap the benefits of intercourse.

However, much more of the advice concerns women, and this emphasis is due to the belief that the woman needed to be sufficiently aroused to produce female sexual essence, which the man could then absorb. This Yin essence, contained in the vaginal fluids, was thought to be infinite, in contrast to the man's vital stock of generative essence (*ching*), which was produced by arousal but lost through ejaculation. To this end the Taoists placed great importance on ejaculation control, urging men to preserve their semen as a fundamental source of life. The texts teach that to satisfy his partner fully without depleting his precious essence, a man must practice "contact without leakage," prolonged intercourse without loss of semen.

The Judeo-Christian Traditions

Lord, love me hard,
love me long and often.
I call you, burning with desire.
Your burning love enflames me constantly.
I am but a naked soul, and you, inside it,
are a richly adorned guest.

MECHTILDE OF MAGDEBURG

At first glance the Christian tradition appears to offer an unremittingly negative attitude toward sexuality and the role of women. In mainstream Church doctrine, sexual intercourse is allowed for the purposes of reproduction, and only when performed within the bounds of marriage. The very close association of sex and sin in Christian theology has led to a deeply unhealthy, unspiritual view of our sexual natures. Women—"the weaker vessels"—have been mistrusted as potential temptresses, because of Eve's culpable role in mankind's fall from grace. From St. Paul's time onward the physical body has been viewed with suspicion, if not downright hostility, leading to feelings of shame and guilt about their natural sexuality among devout Christians, and fear of their ability to feel pleasure.

A major influence on the Church's attitude to sexuality was the writing of St. Augustine of Hippo (354–430 CE). After a dissolute early life, he came to believe that sexual desire was innately evil, and that celibacy presented the only true path to salvation. He argued that Adam and Eve's act of disobedience had corrupted all of nature, and that infants were infected from the moment of conception with the disease of original sin. The Augustinian legacy remains with us today in, for instance, fundamentalist attitudes toward homosexuality and masturbation, and in the practice of celibacy in the Roman Catholic priesthood.

However, even within this predominantly anti-sexual world view, there are glimpses of a fuller, more sensual spirituality. For example, the Song of Songs is an entire book in the Hebrew Scriptures dedicated to human love as a revelation of the divine. It is a dramatic poem, divided into twelve scenes, with three principal characters—the king (Solomon), a beautiful Shulamite maiden, and her lover, a shepherd. The voices are both male and female. The story follows the triumph of true love over worldly inducements, and the powerful yet tender erotic imagery is a moving celebration of sexual love as a gift from God.

The Song of Songs has been interpreted by Jews as an allegory of God's love for Israel, and by Christians as symbolic of Christ's relationship to his followers. For mystics of both traditions, it symbolizes the relationship between the soul and God. However, the Song of Songs is also regarded by some as an overt guide to sexual love, offering instruction on courting, communication, passion, and intimacy.

The Song of Songs influenced the medieval Christian love mystics, who wrote verses in which they imagined their souls as brides and Christ as the bridegroom. The most passionate of these mystics was Hildegard of Bingen (1098–1179 CE). As well as composing ethereal sacred music, which has become well known in recent years, Hildegard wrote and illustrated three great visionary books in which she used erotic imagery to symbolize her union with Christ. Unusually for the times, she saw God's love as feminine, as a life-giving force, and she compared the Trinity to what she saw as the three aspects of sexual intercourse—strength, desire, and action.

How fair is thy love, my sister, my spouse!
how much better is thy love than wine!
and the smell of thine ointments than
all spices! Thy lips, O my spouse, drop as
the honeycomb: honey and milk are under
thy tongue; and the smell of thy garments
is like the smell of Lebanon.

SONG OF SONGS, 4:10

Overleaf "The woman...she gave me fruit of the tree, and I ate." Adam and Eve in Paradise, by Jan Brueghel (1601–78) and Peter Paul Rubens (1577–1640), showing the fateful moment of choice before mankind's fall from innocence and grace.

It is lovely indeed, it is lovely indeed...
I, I am the spirit within the Earth;
The bodily strength of the Earth is my strength;
The thoughts of the Earth are my thoughts;
All that belongs to the Earth belongs to me;

NAVAHO CREATION CHANT OF CHANGING WOMAN

Creation Spirituality

In our own times, the American theologian Matthew Fox has drawn on the mystical and celebratory aspects of Christianity in a mission to revive what he terms "creation-centered spirituality." A former Dominican monk who, because of his radical views, was silenced by the Vatican and later expelled from the Catholic Church, Fox now works as an Episcopalian in California. He teaches a "sensual spirituality" based on the concept of all creation being fundamentally good. Instead of the Augustinian notion of original sin, Fox invites us to see ourselves as being the recipients of God's original blessing of goodness.

Creation Spirituality calls for a fresh injection of joy and ecstasy into the practice of Christianity. It is open and inclusive and happily incorporates elements from Native American shamanism, Christian mysticism, feminist spirituality, gay rights, dance, the arts, and environmental consciousness into its beliefs and practices.

Fox rejects patriarchal exploitation and advocates a return to a maternal form of religion, which would enable us to revere God as Matrix, the Earth as our mother, and the universe as our grandmother. This mother-centeredness, he believes, will allow people of all faiths to come together at a mystical level. He draws heavily on the work of mystics such as Hildegard of Bingen and Meister Eckhart, and argues that every person is potentially a mystic, born full of wonder, and capable of recovering this sense of mystery.

As in Tantra, this feeling of awe and wonder can be accessed through the senses. The senses therefore are gateways, not obstacles, to the spirit, that enable us to go beyond fleeting pleasure to achieving lasting joy. From this perspective, human sexuality can be seen as a blessing to be respected, a power to be honored within ourselves and others. Lovemaking can be a sacramental experience, and an avenue and path to the divine. Accordingly, Fox writes in *Sins of the Spirit, Blessings of the Flesh:* "Given the great powers of generativity and beauty that sex includes, it is difficult to imagine that the Creator would have relegated sexuality to a less than sacred activity. Surely the ecstasy that sexuality gives and receives is evidence of a divine bias in favor of spirit operating through our sexuality."

Kabbalah

The mystical tradition within Judaism known as the Kabbalah is full of sexual symbolism and contains several texts that relate specifically to the importance of sexuality.

The *Sefer ha-Zohar*, or "The Book of Splendor," the great mystical work of the thirteenth century, offers advice on harmonious lovemaking. At its center is the Tree of Life, an image of divine balance, which consists of ten spheres of emanation, or *sefirot*, through which God is manifest in creation. The *sefirot* embody different attributes and form channels of communication with the divine. Male and female *sefirot* counterbalance each other on the Tree. Because man is a microcosm of creation, we are able to influence matters at the higher level, and in this context lovemaking takes on a cosmic role. Performed with a clear spiritual intent, especially on the Sabbath Eve, it becomes a holy act that unites the masculine and feminine *sefirot*, thus reuniting God with his feminine aspect, the Shekhinah, and conferring blessings on the lovers. The Shekhinah is also known as the Sabbath Bride.

This mystical celebration of sexual love is spelled out in a Kabbalistic marriage manual from the period called the *Iggeret ha-Kodesh*, or "The Holiness Letter": "The union of man with his wife, when it is proper, is the mystery of the foundation of the world and its civilization. Through the act they become partners with God in the act of creation. This is the mystery of what the sages said, 'When a man unites with his wife in holiness, the Shekhinah is between them in the mystery of man and woman.'"

The *Iggeret ha-Kodesh* emphasizes the giving of mutual pleasure during sex. It highlights the importance of foreplay, and recommends that the man ensures his wife reaches orgasm first.

Paganism

In witchcraft, sex is a sacred sacrament, an outward sign of inward grace. That grace is the deep connection and recognition of the wholeness of another person. In its essence, it is not limited to the physical act—it is an exchange of energy, of subtle nourishment between people. Through connection with one another, we connect with all.

STARHAWK, THE SPIRAL DANCE

Neo-Paganism is a nature-based spirituality that encompasses the pre-Christian traditions of Wicca, Odinism, Norse, and Druidism. It reveres the Earth as the visible manifestation of the Great Goddess, and encourages sensual enjoyment in her worship. Sexuality is honored as sacred, not feared as evil. Neo-Pagan organizations tend not to discriminate on the basis of sexual orientation. The largest of these, Wicca, celebrates sexual union as a sacred meeting of male and female energies.

Neo-Pagans can practice alone or in groups, and place a great deal of emphasis on ritual. These may include the casting of a magic circle (defining a sacred space by walking a circle in a clockwise direction), calling the quarters (invoking the spirits of the four cardinal directions, associated with the elements air, fire, water, and earth), worshiping the Gods and Goddesses, observing the season, performing sacred drama, magic, or a visualization; and then banishing the circle, bidding farewell to the spirits, and sharing food. Drumming, dancing, and singing may be included. Rituals can take place out of doors, in natural settings, and may be performed sky-clad (naked).

The Great Rite, one of the most sacred acts in the Wiccan tradition, represents the spiritual marriage of the Goddess and the God. This is a fertility rite that focuses on the Earth and on human creativity. During the ceremony, the sacred union is most often enacted symbolically by lowering a ritual dagger, or *athame*, into a chalice, accompanied by a litany emphasizing the role of the God and Goddess in Wiccan mythology and their completion as one divine being. More rarely, this ritual may involve actual sexual intercourse between the high priestess and priest.

The union of energies involved in the Great Rite represents the ultimate coming together of male and female creative forces, and the powerful energy raised is usually aimed at attuning practitioners to the cycles of the Earth and raising their awareness and connection to divinity.

Right Shrine to the Great Goddess in her various guises, with votive offerings left by members attending the annual Goddess Conference at Glastonbury in Somerset, England, in July 2000.

Sex Magick

A path that deals explicitly with sexual energy and power is Sex Magick. Although it draws heavily on esoteric versions of the Jewish Kabbalah, the modern awareness and practice of Sex Magick owes much to its best-known and most influential exponent, Aleister Crowley. Born in 1875, Crowley was a maverick whose no-holds-barred attitude to sex, drugs, and the occult became so notorious that it led to him being dubbed the "wickedest man alive" by the press. He traveled widely throughout the East, and introduced some of the tantric and yoga practices he had studied there into the magickal groups he joined and formed in the West, among them the Order of the Golden Dawn, the "A∴A∴" and the Ordo Templis Orientis. It was Crowley who added the "k" to magic, to distinguish it from the stage "magic" performed by conjurors, and his ideas have formed the basis of the Sex Magick teachings of many new groups since the Second World War.

The goal of all magick is the manipulation of reality in accordance with the will. Magicians will specify a goal, raise energy, and then release it in the desired direction with the aim of manifesting their goal in physical reality. In Sex Magick, the especially powerful and pleasurable force of sexual energy is raised through prolonged sexual arousal and then released at the moment of orgasm.

Sex magicians believe that acts of ritual intercourse can produce a "magickal childe." This is not a child in the physical sense, and the sexual act does not have to take place between a heterosexual couple, or even a couple at all (focused masturbation—monofocal sex—can also produce magickal effects). The magickal childe is an effect on the astral, or spiritual, plane. Sex magicians use magickal rituals to create the magickal childe on the spiritual plane in the belief that it will eventually manifest itself on the physical plane. So a magickal childe, or a deep, heart-felt desire, created on the astral plane will be "born" in the physical world.

The key trigger for creating this magickal childe is holding a thought during orgasm, and the greater the energy generated during the ritual sexual activity, the more likely it is that the desired results, or magickal childe, will be achieved.

In "energetic" Sex Magick, the sexual energy raised during intercourse is directed by the mind toward magickal goals. In "physical" Sex Magick, the sexual fluids produced during a ritual focused on specific goals are regarded as being charged with magickal energy. These fluids (which are, most commonly, male ejaculate) can be used to anoint a talisman or draw symbols on the body.

Do what thou wilt shall be
the whole of the law...
love is the law,
love under will.

ALEISTER CROWLEY

Otherwise they can be absorbed back into the body as a ritual in itself, thereby internalizing the physical result of the magickal ritual.

The "classic" works of Sex Magick, including those by Crowley, can seem unacceptably sexist today, with women generally placed in the position of "assistant" to male magicians. However, there are increasing numbers of women working and writing in this field who are updating the rituals to embrace the mores of the twenty-first century.

Left Tarot card showing Mercury, the solar-lunar hermaphrodite of alchemy, as the Magus or Magician. This contemporary watercolor by Frieda Harris is based on a design by Aleister Crowley.

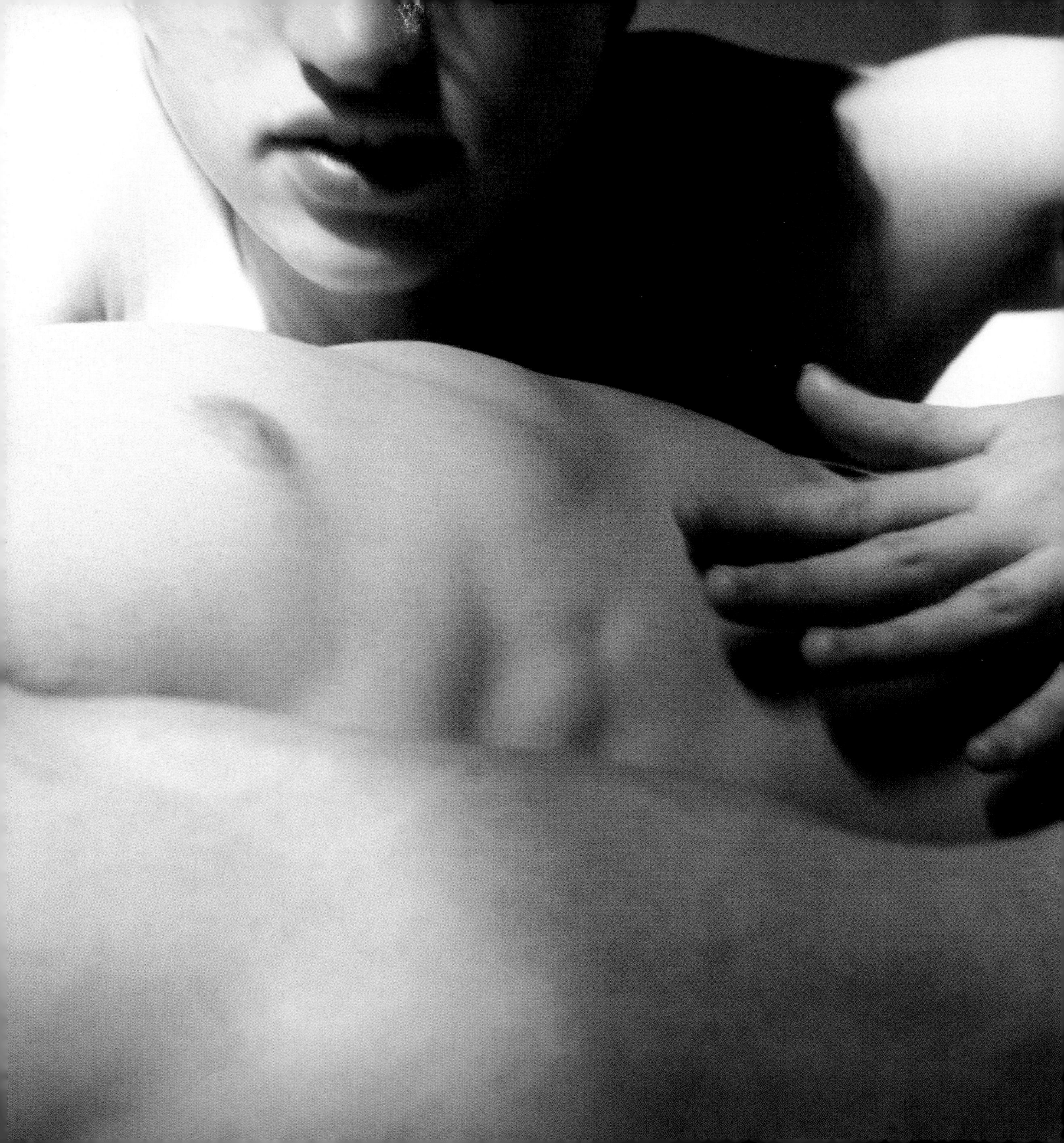

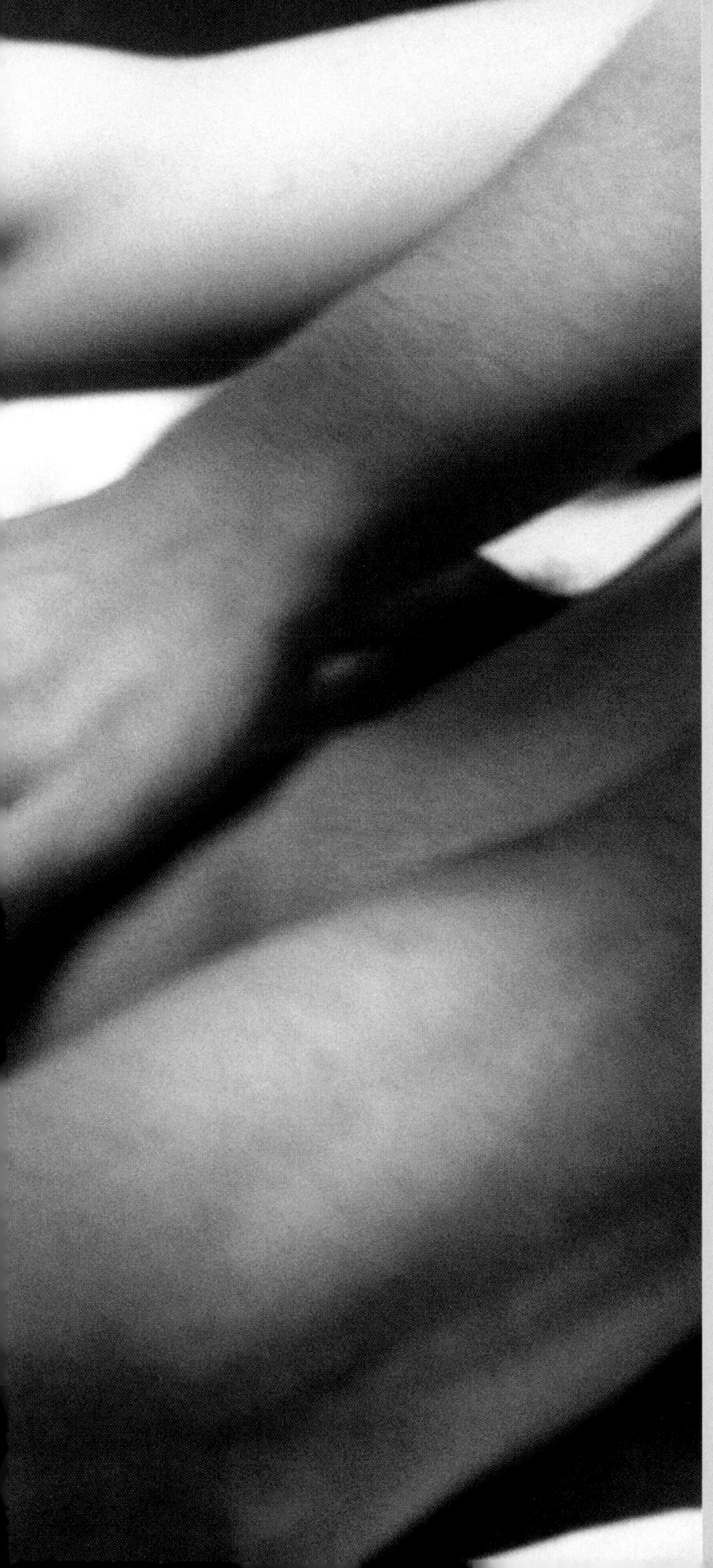

CHAPTER 2

Preparing the Body

Your body is your inner temple, your gateway to the divine, and needs to be treated with the love and respect you would bestow on any holy vessel.

In this chapter we look at the physiology of sex and at its emotional dimension, particularly the need to feel at ease with your body. There are exercises to help you appreciate your sexual needs and responses. What you eat can affect your libido, and we look at foods that enhance your lovemaking. Suppleness and flexibility help to get the most out of sex, and traditional ways to exercise body and mind for optimum well-being are suggested. Rest and relaxation are also covered.

But your inner temple is not just your physical body; it also encompasses the subtle or energy body, and the vortices, or chakras, through which creative energy rises. This can be a difficult concept to visualize, and so exercises are given to raise awareness of your subtle body through the opening and closing of your chakras.

Getting to Know Your Body

There is only one temple in the world,
and that is the human body.
Nothing is holier than this high form.
One touches heaven when one touches a human body.

NOVALIS

Before you try to create sexual magic with a partner it is essential to be comfortable with your own body and its sexual responses. Understanding how your body and sexuality function on a physiological level is the first step.

The next stage, which can be far more challenging, is reaching total acceptance, on an emotional level, of your body as the beautiful and perfect work of art that it is. Exploring the realms of magical sex in the fullest possible way cannot be done hidden under the bedcovers or with the lights turned off—it is a celebration of the potential for ecstasy held within your own body. Love handles, pot bellies, stretch marks, or wrinkles become irrelevant once you are able to recognize and celebrate the miracle of your unique body as a container of the divine.

If you genuinely feel comfortable with your sexual nature you will also feel at ease with your sexual urges and needs. Even today masturbation, or self-pleasuring, remains surrounded by taboo. Few people now believe that masturbation will cause blindness or give them hairy palms, but taking control of your own sexual pleasure can still be an area of shame, particularly for women. As children we were warned not to "play with ourselves down there," reinforcing the impression that our sexual curiosity and instincts were wrong or dirty.

There is nothing shameful about masturbation. It is a natural and highly valuable way of loving yourself and enjoying your body. Rather than being seen as an inadequate "second-best" to sex with a partner, it is a means of celebrating your sexual nature and independence (as well as a valuable adjunct to sex with your lover).

Self-discovery and exploration are essential in getting to know your own responses and needs, whether you have a partner to work with at this stage or not. Learning how to satisfy yourself involves taking control of your sexual pleasure—your orgasm becomes your own responsibility—but you have also gained the knowledge to teach your partner how to satisfy you in the most exquisite ways. The practice of self-pleasuring is also an important way of raising awareness of the subtle energies, and through self-pleasuring you can learn techniques to circulate and direct the flow of energy around the body.

CELEBRATING YOUR BODY

How often do you really look at your naked body? Perhaps rarely with an uncritical and truly appreciative gaze. Try it now. Stand in front of a full-length mirror and celebrate the wonder that is your living, breathing physical self. Turn off your critical gaze and recognize that you are perfect as you are. All that you need is within you.

Stretch up, reaching toward the ceiling. Bend over, toward your toes. Put some music on and dance; rotate your hips and shake your belly; watch and feel how your body moves. Try to cast your mind back to the sense of limitless freedom and curiosity about your body you had as a toddler. Remember how unselfconsciously you would jump, roll, and tumble, exploring movement and space, completely at ease in yourself and free of the inhibitions that developed as you grew up and started to feel social pressures to be a certain shape or size. These pressures become insignificant, even laughable, when you come to understand the power you hold simply through being a sexual being.

If you are a woman, celebrate your womanliness. Revel in your curves and softness and relish your flesh. Run your hands over your body, feeling the weight of your breasts, the roundness of your belly and the curve of your hips. Give your buttocks a good shake; give your whole body a good shake and breathe deeply.

Check you're not still subconsciously holding in your stomach, even just a little, and let the music flow through you. Move your body as you enjoy the beautiful shapes it naturally creates in space. Look at yourself afresh, with awe, and recognize yourself as the archetypal goddess, full of the strength and vulnerability of woman.

If you are a man, reclaim the power of your maleness and recognize yourself as the archetypal god, full of the strength and vulnerability of man. Tune in to your body as sacred, as a vessel of the divine, and feel the natural flow of energy and unique strength running through you. Let yourself go and allow your body to respond to the music. Stroke your chest and belly, running your fingers through your hair. Watch the way the muscles in your shoulders and arms work for you as you lift your arms. Feel loving toward your body, whatever its shape, and celebrate it as the perfect living organism that it is.

Tell yourself that you are sexy. Say it out loud: "I feel sexy." It might be difficult at first and you might feel a bit silly, but just keep repeating it until it becomes second nature and you genuinely feel that you are stating the obvious. Eventually your instinct will react with "Well, *of course* I feel sexy. I *am* sexy!"

SEDUCE YOURSELF

This is an exercise in fully expressing love and confidence in your body and your capacity for sexual joy. You are seducing yourself, being both adorer and adored, a very liberating experience. Allow plenty of time—this is not a quick-fix, but a form of sexual meditation—and make sure you won't be disturbed. Return to this exercise regularly to learn how your responses change. Women may notice changes in feelings of arousal, vaginal color, and wetness over the course of their cycle.

Prepare a warm, inviting, and private space with cushions, candles, and soft music, as if you were awaiting a lover. Gather together some sensual scented oils.

Take a warm bath or long shower until you are completely relaxed, then start to massage scented oil over your whole body. Using different types of stroke—gentle and feather-like or firm and strong—explore how different areas of your skin respond to your touch. Begin to arouse yourself by experimenting with different ways of touching your penis, or clitoris and vagina, and feel all your inhibitions dissolve.

Focus on your whole body and feel the sensations spreading out from your genital area to your thighs, buttocks, and stomach. Caress yourself, exploring your body in the tender and exciting way a lover would. Stroke your nipples and feel the effect it has on your sex center.

Try touching your lips to your arms or shoulders, or blowing down your chest and stomach; stroke your face and run your fingers over your lips. See how your body changes as you get aroused—as nipples become erect, the clitoris or the head of the penis swells and changes color.

Use a mirror to watch yourself. This can be unnerving at first. Persevere—that sense of unease you may experience when you first see yourself fully and joyfully exploring your own sexuality is a barrier to be broken through on the path of celebratory sex.

Get to know the pattern of your sexual response—what feels good, what heightens or diminishes the sensations. As you reach the brink of orgasm, slow down, and get to know the sensation of being just on the edge of orgasm yet able to hold off. Bring yourself to the brink again and again.

After you have finally reached orgasm, carry on treating yourself as a good lover would. Continue to maintain touch by stroking your stomach or wrapping your arms around yourself. Bathe in the afterglow.

The Love Muscle

The pubococcygeous, or PC, muscle is known in Tantra as the love muscle, and exercising and toning it greatly enhances the creation and control of sexual energy.

Awareness of your love muscle helps you to feel more in touch with your body, genital area, and sexual response. You can develop it using simple contraction and relaxation exercises that improve the flow of blood to the region and intensify the build-up of energy during intercourse. A strong love muscle leads to longer-lasting erections and a more sensitive penis. It enables the vagina to grip the penis more intensely, allowing greater control over orgasm, and a more powerful orgasm when you choose to finally go over the edge into ecstatic orgasmic bliss.

In women, this area encompasses the muscles that surround the urethra, vagina, and anus—like a hammock slung from front to back (see page 176). Women often first become aware of it when prescribed pelvic-floor exercises to strengthen the area after childbirth, and to help urine control. In men, the love muscle runs from the base of the testicles to the anus (see page 176).

A good way to identify the muscle, for women and men, is to contract and relax muscles in the area to stop and start the flow of urine. Feel which muscles you use to achieve this, then replicate the action while not urinating.

Women can check whether they have located their love muscle, and test its strength, by lubricating a finger and gently sliding it inside the vagina. Squeeze the love muscle and feel the vagina tighten around your finger; check for a pulling and squeezing sensation as you grip and relax. With practice it will become strong enough to enable you and your partner to make love simply through gripping and releasing the penis as you both lie still, with all the movement taking place internally.

Men will find it easier to control ejaculation, eventually becoming able to ride orgasmic waves without a release of semen, by tightening the muscle while on the brink of ejaculation. For this reason, love-muscle control plays an important role in Taoist sexual teachings, with the view that locking this area, "the gate of mortality," prevents *chi*, the life essence, escaping. Love muscle exercises have the added benefit in men of massaging the prostate gland.

With practice, the exercises on page 40 should take only around five minutes to do, twice a day. The joy of the love muscle work-out is that not only is it pleasurable, it is completely invisible, and can be done anywhere—while traveling to work, sitting at your desk, reading, or watching TV. It is good to turn the work-out into a habit by doing it regularly during your day.

The woman should ever strive to close and constrict the yoni until it holds the lingam as with a finger, opening and shutting at her pleasure, and finally, acting as the hand of the Gopi girl who milks the cow.

ANANGA RANGA

If you are doing your work-out in a private place, you might want to try saying a short mantra or affirmation as you squeeze. Alternatively, simply counting your breath in your head is a good way to ensure that you are not unintentionally holding your breath, and it can introduce a meditational quality to the work-out. Visualizations can also be powerful—try meditating on the energy charge being drawn up the chakras as you squeeze (see pages 56 and 57 for an illustrated description of the chakras).

Try your love muscle exercises during self-pleasuring. For women, the sensation as the vagina tightly encloses and releases their finger can be a highly exciting form of self-exploration, while men can discover how to produce increasingly firm erections through tensing and relaxing all the muscles in the pelvic area and squeezing the base of the penis. At this point men may also want to try "penis bobbing"—raising and lowering the penis through muscle control alone, with a small cloth resting on it. You can gradually increase the weight by wetting the cloth.

Women can also experiment with "weightlifting" exercises by using an object that provides resistance, such as the "eggs" or "balls" sold in some New Age and sex shops. Stone eggs were used in ancient China by the empress and royal concubines to improve their physical and spiritual health. Practicing control of the love muscle with an egg increases its ability to lift sexual energy inward and upward; you can feel the direction of the muscle movement more distinctly through the movement of the egg. With practice, you can move it up and down and from side to side, using muscles in different areas of the vagina. For anyone wishing to try this out, Mantak and Maneewan Chia's book *Healing Love through the Tao* contains information on a number of easy-to-follow egg exercises.

LOVE MUSCLE WORK-OUTS

While the benefits of developing the PC muscle were known in China and India in ancient times, they were introduced to the West in the 1950s by a Los Angeles doctor named Arnold Kegel, and work-outs of this area of the body are known as Kegel exercises. He had initially developed them for patients undergoing surgery for bladder control, but soon found that a wonderful side effect was that the exercises increased orgasmic ability in his clients.

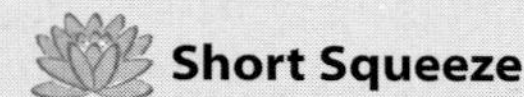

Short Squeeze

Sitting or standing, relax your body, and take a full breath in and a full breath out. Keeping your body relaxed, breathe in and squeeze your love muscle. Breathe out and relax it. Squeeze and relax fully ten times in quick succession, with a "squeeze and relax" roughly every second or faster. Be sure you can feel when the muscle relaxes and when it contracts, and relax fully between contractions. Try to keep the rest of your body at ease, being careful not to clench your abdominal muscles or thighs, or tense your face. Don't forget to breathe!

Aim to build up to a comfortable 75–100 short squeezes twice a day and then add the following variations:

Holding on

Breathing in, squeeze the love muscle, and hold for three seconds. Breathe out and relax fully for three seconds.

Long and Short

Fully contract the love muscle, and hold for ten seconds. At the very end of the contraction, squeeze once rapidly, harder and deeper, then release for ten seconds.

The Slow Movement

Over a period of ten seconds, gradually and slowly contract the love muscle to its maximum, and then slowly reduce the tension over ten seconds.

Food of Love

From purity of food
follows the purity
of the internal organ.

CHANDOGYA UPANISHAD

A lovingly prepared and beautifully presented meal is a delight to all the senses. Taste is arguably the most intimate of our five senses, with its dissolving of the boundaries between subject and object, but food also offers visual satisfaction, olfactory stimulation, and tactile gratification—think of a scented mango or peach, its sweet, overflowing juices and delicate flavor satisfying the palate as silky flesh yields to biting teeth and receptive lips.

In addition to food's capacity to arouse the senses, wise nutritional choices are an essential element of a healthy sex life. Part of the blessing Buddhist monks chant before meals is "We eat to support life," and life force, or sexual energy, is inextricably linked to diet. What we consume affects us physically, emotionally, and mentally. Taoists categorize foods as Yin or Yang and, as in all areas of life, a balance is required in order for the body to work harmoniously. In yogic texts food is classified according to the three Gunas—*Sattva* (purity), *Rajas* (passion), and *Tamas* (inertia)—the same three categories that define the mind in Ayurvedic thought, and Ayurvedic experts prescribe different food combinations for different constitutional types. Generally, for spiritual progress and well-being, a sattvic diet is recommended, consisting of fresh fruit and vegetables, dried fruit, salads, lentils, milk, hazelnuts, almonds, wholegrain rice, and honey.

In nutritional terms, your diet can have a direct impact on your libido. Eating well will make you feel more energetic, for a start, and incorporating libido-boosting foods into your diet can transform your sex life. The hormones that regulate the sex drive—estrogen, progesterone, and testosterone—require niacin (vitamin B3), vitamin B5, vitamin A or beta carotene, and zinc. The B vitamins can be found in milk, yogurt, cheese, fish, and meat, and, important for those on a vegetarian or vegan diet, in green, leafy vegetables, nuts, and dried fruits. Beta carotene is found in carrots, dark-green, leafy vegetables, peppers, apricots, and peaches, as well as other fresh

Overleaf Tantric lovers enjoying the five ritual pleasures that open the doors to rapture. Indian album painting from the late eighteenth to early nineteenth centuries.

yellow, orange, and red fruits. Oysters, that legendary aphrodisiac, are a good source of zinc, but this mineral is also found in hard, crumbly cheeses, brown rice, and offal. It is also a good idea to incorporate foods containing the amino acids tyrosine and arginine into your diet, as these help to produce the neurotransmitters that stimulate alertness and arousal. Protein-rich foods are a good source of these amino acids, as well as high-grade microalgae supplements such as spirulina or chorella.

apple, pear,
gooseberry, banana,
All this speaks death
and life into your mouth.

RILKE

Food and Ritual

As we have seen, in Hindu Tantric practice sacred sex, or *maithuna*, is the conclusion of a long, five-part ceremony whose preliminary stages involve taking *madya* (wine), *matsya* (fish), *mamsa* (meat), and *mudra* (parched grain). All these are thought to be aphrodisiacs, and, in keeping with Tantra's iconoclastic outlook, the first three are ordinarily forbidden to high-caste Hindus.

In the Vaishnava tradition in Hinduism, the practice of devotional surrender is extended even to the preparing and eating of food. Food is offered to the deity with devotion before it is eaten by devotees; this transforms it from material nutrition to spiritual mercy (*prasada*). The preparation of *prasada* becomes an active devotional meditation, undertaken in a peaceful and contemplative atmosphere. Thanks are given for the food and it is eaten with a calm spirit.

A SENSUAL FEAST

Offering your partner a sensual feast, in the spirit of worshiping his or her divinity, is an act of love that prepares the ground for the special time to follow.

Prepare bite-sized foods that can be eaten with the fingers, combining a range of flavors and clean tastes for maximum tastebud stimulation—sweet, sharp, and savory. Avoid high-fat dairy foods that contain tryptophan, which often tend to cause drowsiness. Highly scented fruits, such as mangoes and pineapples, are perfect for their interesting textures and fresh taste.

Think about how to present the offerings in the most enticing way—you may want to use a special plate or tray just for this purpose, decorating it with flowers or fresh herbs.

It can also be exciting to blindfold your partner before feeding them the morsels you have prepared, tantalizing them by brushing each item over their lips and tongue first. Have a glass of chilled water or small ice cubes handy to refresh the palate between different tastes.

Foods that are ideal for ritual offering in a sensual feast, offering a varied mix of tastes and textures, can include the following: asparagus, candied violets, peeled grapes, strawberries, slices of fresh mango, small squares of rich, dark chocolate, olives, and small pieces of sashimi.

Fit for Sex

You don't need to be super-fit to follow the practices suggested in this book, but a certain level of suppleness and flexibility will help you to get the most out of the exercises and positions, as well as generally improve the quality of your health and life. In addition to the physical benefits, regular exercise helps you to feel good about yourself and your body—an essential precursor to open and adventurous sex—and promotes deep relaxation.

The best forms of exercise to prepare yourself for sacred sex are those that work with body and mind. Yoga and tai chi, the movement disciplines associated with Tantra and Taoism respectively, are ideal. Both combine physical exercise with awareness of breath. Through the application of mindfulness they become a moving meditation, integrating form with meaning. These practices increase the flow of energy and act on energy blockages, helping to develop the skills and sensitivity vital to transformational sex. They also increase the ability to be present in the here and now, as they seek to move consciousness into the body and breath, ridding the mind of chatter and the pull to the past or future.

According to legend, tai chi was developed by the thirteenth-century Taoist monk Chang San-Fen. He is said to have witnessed a fight between a snake and a crane that inspired him to create a boxing style imitating the dance of their movements. The crane symbolized universal

When man is born he is soft and flexible;
When he dies he grows hard and rigid.
So it is with all things under Heaven.
Plants and animals are soft and pliant in life,
But brittle and dry in death.
Truly, to be hard and rigid is the way of death;
To be soft and flexible is the way of life.

TAO TE CHING

consciousness, and the snake the regenerative power of nature. Tai chi is now practiced more as an internal art than as a form of self-defense, enhancing mental clarity, natural power, flexibility, and grace, and promoting the smooth flow of energy. The sequences of movements represent the flow and interchange of Yin and Yang and are designed to stimulate the flow of *chi*, the vital life force, along the energy meridians of the body, with the goal of reaching unity of mind and body in movement.

Yoga dates back over five thousand years to the sages of the civilization centered on the cities of Harappa and Mohenjo-daro in the Indus valley, who created a set of physical postures and breathing exercises to stretch, cleanse, and center the body. The Sanskrit word *yoga* comes from the root *yuj*, to unite or to yoke, and refers to the joining of mind and body. As with tai chi, the aim is to attain unity of being through the balance of mind and body. There are, of course, many different schools of yoga and, while Kundalini yoga is the most relevant to Tantric practice, it is important that you find the path that best suits you. Hatha (sun and moon union) yoga is the most widely practiced and is excellent for all-round toning, flexibility, and relaxation. Astanga vinyasa yoga (also known as "power yoga") is gaining in popularity, largely due to its endorsement by high-profile celebrities such as Madonna. Astanga uses a warming breath to move the body through a set series of flowing postures.

Suitable for all ages and levels of fitness, yoga and tai chi require no equipment and can be practiced anywhere. A short daily session of basic exercises can also produce remarkable changes in a relatively short space of time.

There are many good books and videos available on these movement forms, but it is also advisable to take a few introductory classes with a qualified teacher in order to learn the basic postures correctly before you start to practice regularly. If you have any kind of medical condition or concerns, then you must always seek professional advice before embarking on a new form of exercise.

Even if you already have a regular exercise schedule, whether it is going to the gym or swimming pool, cycling to work, or jogging in the park, it is worth considering your frame of mind as you exercise, and introducing a more meditative dimension to the activity. For example, you can visualize the flow of energy around your body as you work out, focus on your breathing, and shift your awareness to a calmer place.

Safer Sex

In choosing a lover
you are choosing your destiny.
MANTAK CHIA

Sex is the source of creation. Unfortunately, it can also be a source of destruction. Sexually transmitted diseases are a potential threat to all sexually active people, and the importance of minimizing risk cannot be emphasized enough.

The power of sex as a sacred act that can heal us but also hurt us echoes the Taoist view that lovemaking can have a profound impact on our health and well-being as well as on our psyche and spirit. Sex should always be viewed as more than an emotional and spiritual exchange between two people—it is also a physical and energetic exchange that needs to be treated with respect and awe.

You alone are responsible for your own health. Respect and honor your body, and those with whom you share it, by informing yourself about the risks of HIV (the virus that causes AIDS) and other sexually transmitted diseases.

Safer sex techniques include the use of condoms to prevent infections that are transmitted through bodily fluids. Use them correctly and with the understanding that even sex with a condom can never be one hundred percent safe.

Many men dislike condoms as they can decrease sensitivity. However, this can also have a welcome side-effect in that it can help men who have a tendency to ejaculate too quickly. In addition, in sacred sex, a slight loss of sensitivity in the penis is far offset by the increased awareness of the potential for the entire body to feel heightened pleasure, and the move away from lovemaking as a purely genitally focused activity.

Be aware of the risk of exchanging fluids by oral sex, and use condoms or dental dams (thin pieces of latex that cover the vulva and act as a barrier against vaginal fluids) if you have any doubts about your partner's sexual health.

Get to know your partner fully before contemplating unprotected sex. Honest communication lays the groundwork for the trust and intimacy required by sacred sex, and if you do not feel comfortable broaching the subject of condoms with your prospective lover, then you should be asking yourself whether you are really ready to share the most physically and mentally intimate act with them.

There are many alternatives to penetrative sex, and some of them are covered in this book. Extended foreplay—touching, stroking, and mutual pleasuring—can be as stimulating as intercourse and still allows for the movement and exchange of energy that is the key to sacred sex.

Rest and Renewal

Your body is more fit
for love than war.
Let heroes wage war;
devote yourself to love
at all times.

OVID

Looking after your body encompasses more than just diet and exercise; it also involves giving your body and mind all the rest and relaxation they need to release built-up tensions. Paradoxically, relaxation holds the key to energy.

Recreational sex can be a wonderful way to unwind, relax, and take your mind off the day's worries. However, when making love in the ways described in this book—raising energy in order to connect with the mystery of creation—it's best to be relaxed before you start. Otherwise, those everyday concerns and stresses will impinge on your concentration, drawing you off the "now" and causing the connection with your partner, and the likelihood of attaining a higher state of consciousness, to suffer. If you are tired before you make love, then the natural instinct is to seek release as quickly as possible—out of the window goes creating a sacred space, focusing awareness, and arousing each other with foreplay. Sometimes, of course, speedy, immediate sex is all you want, or all you can muster, and there's nothing wrong with that—indeed, it has its own benefits. Quick sex need not be rushed sex if you can keep your mind in the moment rather than let it run ahead to the next task. The change of pace provided by quick sex can also create a good sense of balance in your sex life.

However, while sustained, creative erotic union certainly requires more time and energy than "fast-food" sex, it repays the extra effort a thousandfold.

If you have been relying on sex to relax, try to find other ways to calm your mind so that you come to your partner with a fresh outlook and the energy to engage fully in your sacred lovemaking. Think about the times you normally have sex. Is it usually late in the evening, after a long day at work and a heavy meal, when you know you have to be up early again the next morning? Instead, try to shake up your routine and set aside some less pressured time specifically for exploring the realm of sexual magic.

Make a conscious effort to do something that will relax you before making love. If you have been sitting in front of a computer in an airless office all day before traveling home on a packed commuter train, resist the urge to

slump in front of the television for an hour to "relax," and instead increase your energy and reawaken your connection with nature by taking a walk in a park. Do it with your lover and you can both talk through the work battles or family dilemmas of the day, so when you enter your sacred space it is with a clearer mind.

You may also need to spend some time being very quiet and still in order to restore your energy levels and re-center yourself. This can be achieved through a short meditation to refresh and calm your mind, or a warm, deep bath to soothe aching muscles, relax the body, and nurture the psyche.

SURRENDERING IN SAVASANA

The "corpse" posture in yoga, savasana, is a deeply relaxing pose that is normally taken at the end of a yoga session. It is also an effective way of letting go at any time.

Lie flat on your back with your legs together. Check that your body is balanced—the top of your head, center of your heart, and touching heels should be in a straight line. Let your toes drop outward, away from each other.

Keep your arms close to your body, lying by your sides with the palms facing up. Fully relax your shoulders so that your upper back can settle down flat on the floor. Relax your arms and soften your fingers and thumbs. Soften and lengthen the back of your neck, allowing it to extend up toward the crown of your head.

Keeping your eyes gently closed, relax the muscles of your face, and breathe in, deeply and slowly, through your nostrils. Exhale fully and feel your body soften and melt inward. As you breathe in and out, keep listening to your breath.

Starting with your feet and working your way up to the top of the head, bring your attention to each part of your body, consciously relaxing it before proceeding on to the next. It can help to direct your mind to each part in turn, telling it to "relax, let go."

First, focus on your toes, bringing your awareness right into each toe in turn. Then, shift your attention to your instep and heel, and up into your ankles. Slowly move up your legs—calves, knees, and thighs—and to your buttocks, pelvis, and hips. Some areas might take longer than others but don't rush

One of the biggest passion-killers, especially for those with children, is lack of sleep. Take a look at your sleep patterns. Are you getting enough? Adequate sleep is essential for renewal, but it is often one of the first things to go when life is busy. If you have trouble sleeping, avoid heavy meals, alcohol, and caffeine for at least two hours before bedtime. A relaxing activity—such as meditation, or the yoga exercise below—an hour before you go to bed, a warm bath, and a few drops of oil of lavender on your pillow can aid sleep. If you get a mid-afternoon slump, a "power-nap"—ten to fifteen minutes' snoozing—is an instant re-charger that doesn't affect your ability to sleep at night.

this process. Instead, savor the feeling of becoming aware of every part of your body as the tension and defensiveness you have been holding within it dissolves.

Continue to move your attention up the length of your body, focusing on your ribs and your chest as it rises and falls with your breathing. Take time over your shoulders, a common store of tension, and then move down your arms—upper arms, elbows, forearms, wrists, knuckles, fingers, and thumbs. Try stretching your hands out and clenching your fists before relaxing them fully. Now place your awareness on your back and let it soften and release right across its length and breadth. Move your mind up your spine, and across your shoulder blades. Let your neck soften, and finally your face. Check for tension around your mouth, cheeks, eyes, nose, and temples, and allow it all to relax and let go.

As your whole body gradually softens and relaxes, feel yourself sinking into the earth in a gradual process of release and descent. Your senses will be drawn inward as your body feels as if it is merging with your surroundings until you lose the distinction between inside and outside. Continue to listen to your breath, and watch over the quiet pool of stillness you have become.

Remain in *savasana* for at least ten to fifteen minutes and emerge from this state gently. Wiggle your fingers and toes to begin the reawakening of your body before stretching out and rolling onto your right side. When you feel ready, open your eyes and gradually rise to a sitting and then a standing position. Enjoy the feeling of complete refreshment and renewal.

The Subtle Body and its Energy Centers

In Tantric and Taoist thought we have a subtle or etheric body that animates and permeates our physical body. Most of the time we are unaware of our subtle body, so this can be a tricky concept to grasp. One way to think about it is to regard the physical body as being only the densest form of our body's energy, part of a continuum of variable energy intensities. The subtle body is not a separate state, but rather a different point on the spectrum, just as both radiation and electricity are different aspects of energy.

Our subtle body draws on the vital life force around and within us. This invisible energy, which flows through the universe, binds our physical and subtle bodies, nourishing, replenishing, and attuning us, and bringing us into harmony with the universe.

Spiritual techniques and practices that focus on awareness of the life force and its journey through our bodies help us to reach a state of mental calm and heightened awareness, in which it becomes easier to shift our attention from the physical to the more subtle aspects of the body.

In Tantric thought, our personal energy, known as Kundalini, may be visualized as a sleeping serpent, coiled at the base of the spine, ready to be awakened and drawn upward to create powerful states of spiritual ecstasy. Through sex, this Kundalini energy can be guided and used to increase vitality, awareness, and, ultimately, to allow us to connect with the energy of the universe. Kundalini is female, Shakti power, able to create and destroy. It rises up the body through the vital energy centers, or chakras, to unite with the inner Shiva (located in the crown of the head) in order to complement it in cosmic union, triggering bliss-consciousness or *samadhi*, the realization of the true Self beyond the ego.

When Kundalini energy is awakened, it travels up the subtle body through a central channel, passing through each chakra in turn. This central channel, or inner flute, is known as the *sushumna.* It corresponds to the spine and connects the main chakras, each of which represents a stage of spiritual refinement in the ascent of the power.

The chakras (meaning "circle" or "wheel" in Sanskrit) are energy vortices, whose role is to refine and transform our raw sexual energy into spiritual illumination. There are, broadly speaking, three views of these vital nerve centers. The first is biological, and locates each chakra in a corresponding physical organ. The second ascribes them to the subtle or etheric body, while the third regards them as purely symbolic, indicating concentration points for focusing meditation. All three interpretations, however, regard the chakras as junctions of life energy, interfaces

between heaven and Earth, that are driven by consciousness. They generate a field of force, and when we work with the energy body by rebalancing ourselves through our chakras, we allow energy to begin to flow freely, and clear the path for the journey of spirit.

The chakras are positioned within the body, from the base of the spine to the crown of the head. Their number may vary according to each tradition, but all the systems have evolved from the Hindu fivefold view of the paths to enlightenment. In mainstream tradition there are seven.

Some tantric practitioners consider the upper three chakras—throat, third eye, and crown—to be as one. It should also be remembered that the traditional classification is not definitive. According to one view, there is an infinite number of chakras; wherever consciousness is placed, a chakra is awakened. So, depending on the focus of consciousness, different chakras come into existence.

Chakras cannot be seen, but they can be sensed. Awareness of them can be raised through psycho-physical techniques and exercises such as visualizations and meditation. They can be visualized as lotus flowers—each associated with a particular psychological or spiritual function, with an element, and with a *mantra* (power word).

The seven chakras of Kundalini yoga with their associated symbols and mantras are as follows:

Muladhara (root support)

The first chakra is located at the base of the spine. It is the home of sleeping Kundalini energy, the creative force of the cosmos, and governs our instincts. It represents primordial need and survival. Its element is earth, and its mantra is *lam.*

Svadisthana (abode of the self)

This is the sacral or pelvic chakra, and its element is water. It governs pleasure, fertility, desire, and *tattva* (taste), and is the chakra for assimilation of raw experiences. Its mantra is *vam.*

Manipura (to shine like a jewel)

The solar plexus or navel chakra is transformatory and is associated with love, healing, and personal power. Its element is fire, its mantra is *ram.*

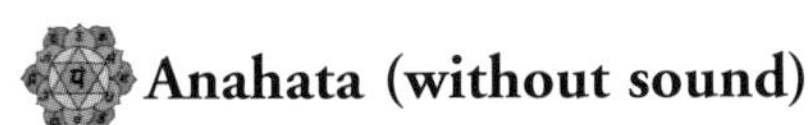

Anahata (without sound)

The heart chakra is the bridge between body and consciousness, and its element is air. It governs altruistic love and compassion, and the ability to surrender. It is emotional, mystical, and unpredictable. Its mantra is *yam.*

Visshuda (purified)

Communication and creativity are associated with the throat chakra, as well as inhalation, exhalation, and balance. Its element is ether or space, and its mantra is *ham.*

Ajna (command from above)

The "third eye" is the bridge between the higher and the lower mind and represents perception, clairvoyance, and intellect. It is associated with light and its mantra is *om.*

Sahasrara (thousand-spoked)

The crown chakra is the home of the divine, of union and wisdom. It is cool and mystical, and has no associated element or mantra.

OPENING THE CHAKRAS

Working with the chakras and becoming aware of the movement of the life force in our bodies helps us to move beyond thinking of sex as a purely physical activity to one that encompasses the heart and spiritual realm. This exercise can be done fully clothed or naked. Lie down in a warm, comfortable space, and create a meditational mood with low lighting or soft music.

Focus your attention on the base, or root chakra, and visualize a glowing, pulsating sphere of red light. See it. Sense it. Experience its pure, scintillating energy. Repeating its mantra, *lam*, should make it glow even brighter. Visualize the circle of light and energy expanding so that it encompasses the whole of your lower spine.

Draw more energy into the area until you feel it spiraling, like a snake, and starting to rise. As it reaches your stomach, feel the energy spinning into another hub of energy, this time of bright orange light. Repeat the mantra *vam*.

As the energy continues to spiral upward it pools into another circle of pure light—the bright yellow solar wheel or plexus. Visualize it as a golden, spinning sun in your navel region. Chant the mantra *ram*.

Feel more energy rising up from the base of the spine and draw it further in and up the spine until it reaches the center of your chest—the heart chakra. The green glow in this area should be spinning rapidly, shining brightly so that it spreads out to cover the whole of your chest. See and feel it filling your chest with warm, green light. Chant the mantra *yam*.

Renew the energy from the root chakra and feel it rising up again, away from your chest to your throat. Visualize it in the form of a blue, spinning sphere right at the center of your throat. At this stage, repeat the mantra *ham*.

Once again, draw your attention to the base of the spine and recharge the energy, still glowing and spiraling, and bring it spinning up through the sacral, solar, heart, and throat chakras until it reaches the middle of your forehead—the third eye. Visualize a pool of pure violet energy pulsating just behind the bridge of your nose, and chant the mantra *om*.

Draw the energy up once more, but this time, as the violet sphere spins faster and faster, feel it rise up out of the crown of your head in a fountain of pure white light, bathing your body in revitalizing energy.

Feel the warmth and power of the energy enveloping you. Recharge the energy by going back to the base of your spine and drawing more back up through each chakra before letting it cascade downward again. Repeat this three times, then relax.

As you do this exercise, some chakras may feel easier to open than others. Relax and breathe into those that you find more difficult, rather than tensing up with effort. As you go through the chakras, try placing your hands over the area of each one in turn to help you to focus and reinforce the flow of energy. You can recharge the energy by repeating the mantra of each chakra as it is reached.

CLOSING THE CHAKRAS

The root and crown chakras should be left open after this exercise, but the others should be closed again, using the following method.

Find a "closing off" image that works well for you—you might visualize a shutter over a beautiful stained glass window, an eyelid over an eye, or a flower drawing in its petals before nightfall, for example. Now, draw white light down from the crown chakra so that it covers your whole body. As it pours down over your third eye chakra, let it act as a trigger for your closing visualization, slowly and gently closing off the chakra.

Again, free a cascade of white light downward, which then passes the (shut) third eye. Carry on down, "shutting" your throat chakra on the way.

Repeat this so that each chakra in turn—heart, solar, and sacral—is closed, but not forgetting to leave the root chakra open to absorb energy.

The Taoist Subtle Body

Taoists believe that life is governed by the Three Treasures, which relate to body, mind, and spirit, and are located in an individual's three elixir fields, or *tan t'iens.*

Ching, or essence, is the fundamental energy of the body, associated with growth and organic change, and is located in the pelvic area. *Chi* is the vital energy of existence, able to move and activate, and is situated in the middle *tan t'ien,* around the solar plexus. *Shen,* best translated as Spirit, is associated with human consciousness. It is located in the upper *tan t'ien,* in the head, and is our highest level of awareness.

Taoists seek to transform essence into energy, energy into spirit, and spirit into the stillness of the Tao. This is achieved by raising energy upward, from the pelvis to the crown. *Chi* passes through energy meridians that are similar to the chakras, although they do not correspond exactly. On reaching the top of the head, the *chi* descends down the front of the body to form a complete orbit—"the circulation of the light."

The path along which energy travels is called the microcosmic orbit and it consists of two channels—one that goes up the spine and another that runs down the front of the body. The two channels are connected by the tongue, and touching the tongue against the front part of the roof of the mouth closes the circuit. Sexual energy, or *ching,* can be drawn up these channels and circulated around the body.

The microcosmic orbit uses controlled breathing and visualization. On inhaling, *chi* is directed from the lower *tan t'ien* in the abdomen down to the perineum, then guided up the back through the tail bone, along the back meridian, and up and over the top of the head. On exhalation, the energy is guided toward the front of the body through the third eye point and down the front channel of the body, back to the lower *tan t'ien.*

A major difference between the Taoist and Tantric views on the circulation of sexual energy is that in Taoist thought, the energy that is circulated to the brain should always be brought back down to the abdomen, where it is stored. Taoists believe that while the head is superb at transforming and projecting energy, it is not a good place to hold it. The organs in our abdomen, however, are ideal for this purpose as they have the capacity to release energy to the body as it is needed. In addition, the abdomen contains a complex neural web, regarded by Taoists as a "second brain" from which many feelings originate. This might sound rather odd, until you think how often you act according to "gut instinct."

CHAPTER 3

Preparing the Mind

Practicing transformational sex requires the cultivation of mind, body, and spirit. It is not enough to immerse ourselves in the physical experience. In order to appreciate its full sensuality we need clarity of mind as well, and then to anchor the experience in the divine.

At the very heart of the unfiltered sense experience of sacred sex is the feeling of just "being"—free from distracting thoughts and fully alive in the present moment. An incredible sensation of melting and dissolving, of going beyond the self occurs, and those moments can be enhanced by developing the ability to lift our minds above the pull of the past and future. Meditation is one of the best ways to achieve this, and we look at Eastern and Western meditation techniques.

However calm and clear your own mind may feel, lovemaking with a partner necessarily involves two minds, and so we also look at techniques for attuning yourselves to each other, so that you are both in flow with the shared vibrations of your minds and bodies.

Meditation

If the thoughts are absolutely tranquil
the heavenly heart can be seen.
The heavenly heart lies between the
sun and the moon
[between the two eyes].
It is the home of the inner light.

LU YEN

Meditation is an ancient and universal approach to self-realization. Based upon personal experience rather than intellect or theory, it is open to anyone willing to do it. It has a long history in both Eastern and Western religions, although most Westerners would probably now associate it with Eastern spirituality. In today's "spiritual supermarket" there is a bewildering array of meditation schools, traditions, practices, and techniques on offer. What they all have in common, however, is the stress on self-awareness, self-knowledge, and self-realization, and they all utilize the beam of attention. The practice of meditation brings transformation at every level—physiological, psychological, emotional, and ultimately, spiritual—leading eventually to the awakened state that is enlightenment.

Meditation practice usually involves concentrating on an object—a flower, candle, mystical diagram, sound, or breath. In Zen meditation a paradoxical statement called a *koan* is sometimes used. The best known of these is the classic question "What is the sound of one hand clapping?" An answer is not expected. The point of the *koan* is to knock down the barriers of normal modes of thinking.

These devices are used to focus our attention in order to distance us from our usual stream of chaotic consciousness. Over time, the stream of random thoughts arising during meditation diminishes. More importantly, our attachment to these thoughts, and our identification with them, is progressively reduced. As we meditate we may drift off or get caught up in a recurring thought pattern, but once we become aware of this, we are gently brought back to the object of concentration.

Meditation involves sitting quietly, allowing the mind to switch off and be still as you calm your inner chatter and allow thoughts to pass through without holding or evaluating them. This is an active process that cleanses the mind and allows the body to relax. It has well-documented physiological benefits—reducing blood pressure, lowering the pulse rate, increasing oxygen intake, and offsetting stress—but regular meditation is most appreciated for its mental effects. It allows our inner mental maelstrom to settle, resulting in the mind becoming more peaceful, calm, and focused. In essence, meditation allows our awareness to become rejuvenated.

The value of regular meditation practice for our well-being in general, and for a refreshed outlook on lovemaking in particular, is recognized by all sex-positive traditions. It may, at first sight, seem odd to associate the quiet stillness of meditation practice with the heightened sensations and pleasures of lovemaking. However, learning to focus your mind in this way will enable you to bring that meditative awareness to lovemaking, so that you are truly focused on those sensations, and on your connection with your lover, rather than the myriad other things going on in your life. The combination of mindful calmness and clarity enhances your sexual experience, allowing you to be fully alive in the moment of bliss, and taking your awareness and energy to new heights.

As you reach new highs during sacred sex, meditation has an additional benefit. It provides you with the skills to ground these highs and integrate them into everyday life. In this way, your sacred sexual experiences become more than a number of peak moments; they begin to form a continuous thread of bliss and clarity in your life.

Starting to Meditate

While the ultimate goal of meditation is common to the different schools and traditions, there is, we have seen, a great variety of meditation techniques, and you need to find one that is right for you. Some people choose to meditate in a group, finding that the discipline of a fixed schedule and the energy of being around other people in an intense state of stillness is helpful. Others prefer to use "guided meditation" tapes or have gentle music playing. Some people require absolute silence, or find that the quality of their meditation improves if they are out of doors in a peaceful, natural setting.

However you choose to meditate, the most important part of your practice is that it is just that—a regular practice. Set aside about twenty minutes a day (or ten to fifteen minutes if you are just beginning), ideally at the same set time. Many people find that the early morning, before the hustle and bustle of the world starts up, suits them best.

Be patient with yourself—the ability to remain in meditative thought for even a few seconds takes time and practice. Remember also that meditation need not only happen when you are purposefully engaged in your daily practice. Any activity can become a meditation if it is performed with awareness, and the sexual act is one that benefits greatly from a meditative consciousness. Learning to become more fully present in the "now" during love-making means that your attention is based purely in the sensation of the moment—the feel of your partner's lips, the sound of their breathing, the energy moving between you. This level of awareness will be cultivated through your meditation practice, but can also be achieved by drawing your thoughts continually to the moment—the here and now—and bringing your meditative awareness into play while you are in erotic union with your lover and fully focusing on the sensations passing between you.

MEDITATION

Choose a quiet place where you will not be disturbed by the telephone, visitors, your partner, or children. Meditation is traditionally done cross-legged or kneeling on the floor, but you can just as well sit in a chair with both feet firmly on the ground. If you decide to use an object to focus your meditation, place it in front of you in a position that allows you to gaze at it without straining.

Relax your body, then scan it mentally to release all tensions. If need be, tense and relax the whole body, or those specific areas in which you habitually store up tension. As you do this, let your breathing become calm and peaceful.

Now, start to turn your attention inward. Disengage yourself from any distractions around you and begin to detach yourself from any thoughts that may arise. Concentrate on the object you have chosen.

Empty your mind of all thoughts. Then bring your chosen object before your inner mind's eye. Don't allow the mind to jump to another object or thought. Let any thoughts that arise pass through without holding or following them.

Calmly and patiently, ease your attention back to your object of focus. Don't force your mind—it will immediately strain to do the opposite—but take an easy, gentle approach. Cultivate a feeling of stillness.

Visualization

Just as a clear gem is colored by the color of other objects around it, so also is the gem of the mind colored by the constructive imagination.

ARYADEVA

Visualization is a meditative technique that uses the power of the imagination to train the mind and manifest goals. It is like running a mental movie or picture through your mind's eye, in which specific positive outcomes, images, or stories are conjured up and played out in detail, and then allowed to become ingrained in your consciousness. Visualization has been used by sports people to "see" themselves winning races, for example, and by patients to stimulate the body's own healing mechanism.

In Tantra, visualizations are used to "refill" the mind with a renewed focus on each of the senses when experiencing the bliss that arises out of the emptiness of meditation. It harnesses the power of the imagination to develop inner vision, rather than inner dialog. In order to relate the microcosm of the mind to the macrocosm of the universe, Tantric practitioners may visualize a whole natural scenery inside their minds and bodies, filling them with mountains, valleys, trees, rivers, and volcanoes. In this way the life force of the outer world can enter the inner world of the body through the power of the mind.

Erotic visualization is also an important part of Tantric teaching, which uses colors and symbols to reduce the mind's reliance on verbal explanations. Thus, a sensual goddess might be visualized as the color red, blazing with the fires of lust. These concentrated visual thoughts are regarded as truly eternal, and as vehicles of liberation.

Visualizing your own lover as an erotic god or goddess is a good way to hold their inherent divinity in mind during day-to-day reality. Build up a picture of them in intricate and loving detail as they dance before you in your mind's eye, perhaps colored passionate red, wearing symbolic ornaments, and garlanded with flowers.

Overleaf Krishna, the divine warrior-hero of the sacred Ramayana epic, with his maidens. His passionate love affairs with the cowherd girls, called Gopis, is a favorite theme of Tantric art. Pahari School, c. 1675–1730.

ANCIENT TANTRIC VISUALIZATION

This visualization for awakening and enhancing the senses is translated from the Chakrasambhara Tantra, a sacred Buddhist text from the sixth to eighth centuries that is believed to contain teachings of the female Buddhas. This translation is by Nik Douglas from his book Sacred Secrets: The Alchemy of Ecstasy.

"Find a quiet place and take up a comfortable position. Contemplate the inherent voidness of all phenomena and recognize that consciousness and blissfulness are to be found within the inner space. Visualize rays of light emerging from the heart center; these rays proceed through the body and reach out into space, shedding light on everything they encounter. Draw back the rays and gather them within; draw in the male and female breaths of the right and left and focus them in the region of the heart chakra. Imagine yourself filled with heroism, fearless, and visualize a lineage of Tantric teachers above your head. Pray to them to aid the process of inner awakening and imagine a red and white disk resting on the junction of nerves in the heart chakra. On that disk imagine a point of light the size of a sesame seed and fix your mind intently on it. Regulate the breath, balancing the left and right until a gentle balance prevails. Hold the mind firm, so it doesn't run astray, and a blissful clarity will result. Then transfer the imagination to the other sense organs.

Imagine two very fine bright white points within the pupils of the eyes. Close the eyes and imagine that the points are still there, and, when the mind is accustomed to it, focus on various objects, all the while keeping the bright points of light before the mind. With practice, the points will be ever more vivid, no matter what the eye falls upon. Having attained stability, draw in the points within the cavern of the heart and imagine the heart gaining brilliancy and clarity. Next, transfer the imagination to the two ears.

Imagine a fine blue point inside each ear and meditate on them, in a totally quiet place. When you have succeeded in fixing the mind upon them, move to a place where there are sounds, but always keep the mind fixed on the two fine blue points. With practice, the points will be more vivid, no matter what one hears. Having attained stability, draw in the points and focus them in the heart chakra. Then transfer the imagination to the nose.

Imagine a fine yellow point inside each nostril and meditate on them in a place free from odors. Concentrate the mind on them and, when the visualization does not waver, move to another place where there are odors. Keep the mind focused on the two fine yellow points, no matter what, and they'll become more vivid. Having attained stability, draw them in the heart chakra. Next transfer the imagination to the tongue.

Imagine a fine red point at the root of the tongue and meditate on it without tasting anything. Concentrate the mind on the red point and, when the visualization is steady, taste some different flavors. No matter what you taste, keep the mind focused on the point so it becomes more brilliant. Once stability is attained, draw it into the heart chakra.

Transfer the imagination to the body and focus on a fine green point at the sexual region, between the anus and the sexual organ. Fix your mind on it, without touching anything. When the mind has attained concentration on the green point, try touching various things, all the while keeping the mind focused so the point becomes even more brilliant. When vividness is attained, stabilize the concentration and draw in the point to the heart chakra.

Mix the different-colored effulgent points within the heart chakra and imagine them dissolving into one another and, finally, into nothingness. Then rising up from the state of Innate Tranquillity, imagine the colored points emerging simultaneously and spontaneously, reaching out and extending to the sense organs. By meditating thus, the whole being becomes purified and the sense exalted. This visualization evolves out of voidness, recedes into voidness, yet is truly filled with the conscious being-bliss experience. ”

Mantra

There are two ways of contemplation on Brahma,
the Original Source.
These are in sound and in silence.
By sound we go to silence.
The sound of Brahma is "OM."
At the end of "OM"—we go to silence.

MAITRI UPANISHAD

In Eastern thought, the whole universe is made up of sound. It is said to have evolved from a single sound that scattered into fifty different vibrations as it expanded outward. Mantras are sacred sounds whose potent vibrational energy is used to aid concentration in meditation, breathing practices, ritual, and lovemaking. The chanting of mantras focuses and protects the mind; their harmonizing vibrations can be used to replace negative thoughts with positive ones.

As we have seen, in Tantric meditation each chakra has its associated Sanskrit power word. There are also "seed syllables"—primordial sound vibrations—that represent spiritual intention. These include:

Hrm – seed of Shakti
Klim – seed of desire
Krim – seed of union
Shrim – seed of delight
Hlim – seed of protection

The supreme mantra is "OM." This is the original sound of the Creator, and the spontaneous vibrational sound of the universe. "OM" is pronounced in three parts—"A" (AH), "U" (OO), and "M" (MM)—with the first syllable quite short, the second longer, and the third longer still, until the sound dies away completely. Carefully and completely uttering "OM" has a purifying effect on the self.

You can use mantras during meditation and love-making. You can also chant a mantra together with your beloved before making love in order to create harmonious

Above, left The traditional symbol for "OM" is an emblem of a sun and moon below a flame, above its written form in Sanskrit or Tibetan. This represents male and female polarities in union.

vibrations between you. The mantra "Om Mani Padme Hum" is ideal when approaching sex as an ecstatic meditation because of its potent, calming, yet energizing influence. Prolong the sounds so that it becomes "Ohhmmm Muhnee Paahdmay Ho-ummm" and it will create a resonance that touches all levels of consciousness. In addition to its wonderful sound, this mantra has a beautiful meaning—"the jewel in the lotus," or "male within the female organ"—signifying sexual union and a blissful state of completeness, of energy infusing wisdom.

Mantras are traditionally received from a teacher or guru, but you may choose to create your own, one that will have a particular significance for you. The power of your mantra could stem from its meaning (perhaps a positive affirmation such as "We are one," or "We are love"), or from the vibrational resonance of its sound (try "Hoo" or "Yumm"). Ideally, your personal mantra should encompass both sound and meaning.

Yantra

Each mantra has a visual equivalent known as a yantra. The archetypal mantra is our breath, with our body as its yantra. The sacred sounds are represented by simple geometric designs that are used as aids in meditation.

Yantras are usually square in shape, with a T-shaped projection on each side representing a gateway. The rectangle frames an inner circle filled with geometric patterns containing a wealth of symbolism. In the center is the *bindu*, an energy dot that signifies the seed—source of creation and supreme consciousness. This is set inside a downward-pointing triangle, symbolizing the yoni. Together they give rise to interpenetrating triangles, representing the subdivisions of the original creative energy into the complexities of creation.

With their geometric patterns, yantras are quite easy for even the most artistically challenged to create. Drawing and coloring in a yantra for your sacred space can be a satisfying meditative act in itself. When you visualize the yantra with your partner before making love, you both become part of it. Ritual sexual positions that create particular shapes with your bodies are also called yantras. These are discussed on page 162.

Another meditative diagram used in Tantric art and ritual is the mandala. These are circular symbolic images that are more complex and detailed than yantras and signify wholeness and totality. Their creative healing power has been used in psychotherapy. The term mandala can also refer to the yoni, as it means an enclosed sacred space.

Mudras

Left A modern Shri yantra from Nepal, c. 1960. This powerful diagram is a condensed image of the whole of creation. Tantrics use it in their daily practice to raise energy and awareness.

The circle within the rectangle represents the cycle of life. The downward-pointing triangles represent Shakti energy and the upward-pointing triangles, Shiva energy. The forty-two goddesses within the circle all represent spiritual attainments.

At the gateways and corners are the eight major deities of the Hindu pantheon; inside each corner, flanked by offerings, a divine protector guards the sanctity of creation.

Mudras are ritual gestures—a direct and potent way of awakening and communicating with the deities within. Placing one's hands together with palms touching in a prayer position is familiar to us all, but in Tantra a whole system of such gestures has evolved. They are used to aid concentration and channel subtle energy, and are thought of as seals—one identifies with the deity, then seals those energies in the body through the ritual hand yantra.

The yoni is represented by placing the hands together, palms upward, so that the inside edges of both hands touch each other.

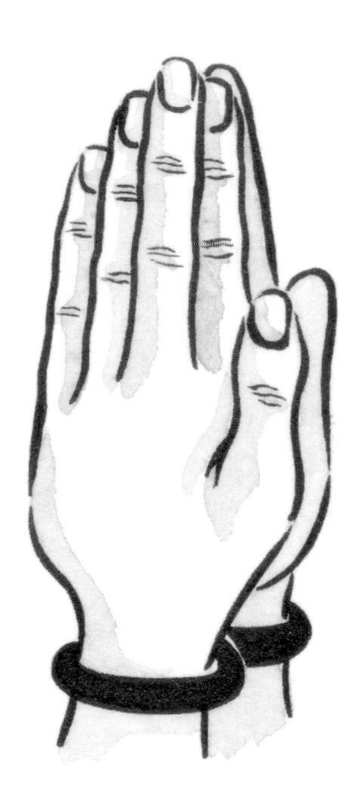

The palms-together mudra of the greeting "Namaste" signifies humility. It literally means "I honor you as an aspect of God."

The lingam mudra has the left hand out flat, inside edge parallel to the body, with the right hand resting on it in a "thumbs-up" gesture, thumb pad facing away from the body.

Symbols in Sex Magick

In Western Sex Magick, mystical symbols known as sigils are often used to focus the mind on one's desires. A sigil is a graphical representation of a magical goal that is charged with power, then imprinted on the subconscious mind.

The English artist and magician Austin Osmon Spare (1888–1956) disliked the elaborate formality of the magical systems devised by Aleister Crowley. He sought to reduce Sex Magick to the bare minimum, and popularized a system of transforming a stated goal or vision into a symbol by compressing letters of the alphabet. The resulting sigil appears visually to be unrelated to the original words of the goal. While this may at first seem counter-intuitive, the unfamiliar look of the sigil allows the conscious mind to be bypassed, and so prevented from blocking the passage of the symbol to the subconscious. The conscious mind is, in effect, "tricked" into not interfering with the vision when the symbol is charged with power and internalized. The creation of the vision on the spiritual plane, with which the subconscious mind is linked, is then believed to lead to its manifestation on the physical plane.

Creating a sigil is a powerful way to clarify your thoughts about your desires, and to give free rein to your artistic instinct. Be bold in articulating your desires, then be equally bold in designing a sigil that will really impact upon your subconscious. Try not to be constrained by any preconceived notions of what a sigil should look like—simply have fun creating something unique.

Let your mind play with shapes and colors. Create a round sigil if it pleases you. If your desire relates strongly to one of the four elements, incorporate a color associated with it. For air, use yellow or gold; for earth, green, black, or brown; for fire, red; and for water, blue or green. With your concentration fully in the moment while designing this abstract representation of your deepest desire, your actions will take on a meditative quality.

Creating a vision and symbol with your lover, and then charging it together during lovemaking, is a powerful and intimate act. Your sigil could be made with a goal focused on a specific session of lovemaking, or it could symbolize your shared vision for your long-term union. Integrate it into your lovemaking, pausing during your sexual dance to gaze at it in your mind's eye, or place it in a position where you can both see it during sex. Again, on reaching climax, visualize it deeply, anoint the material manifestation with your sacred sexual fluids, and then finally, bury it.

Right Nude Holding a Crystal Ball, by Austin Osmon Spare, 1914–20. Spare was an occultist who would draw while in a trance.

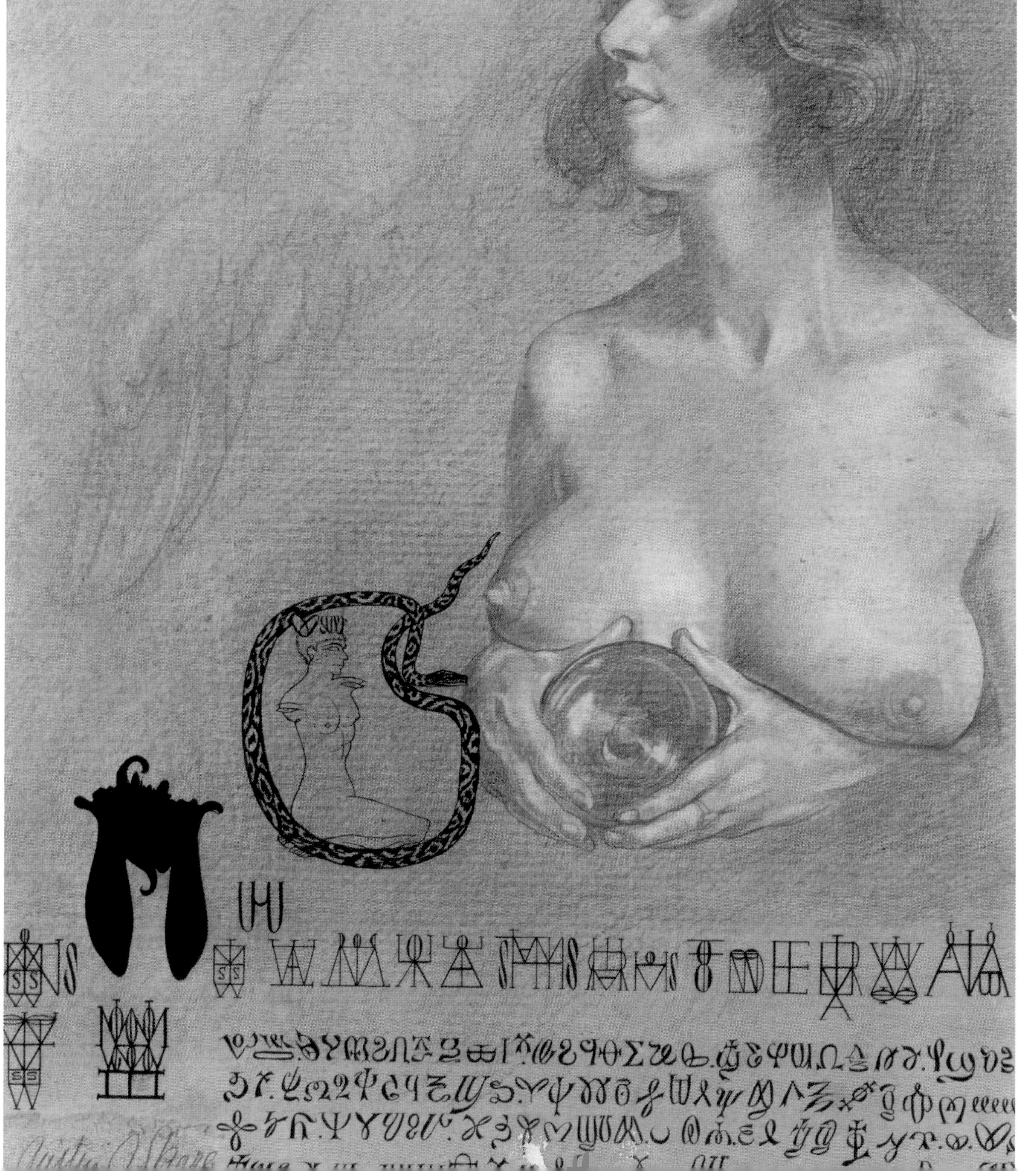

CREATING A SIGIL

First, visualize your goal fully. It might be material, such as a better job; emotional, such as a wish for greater happiness in life; or sexual, say, the enjoyment of better orgasms. Think your vision through completely, without rushing, and incorporate all your senses into it. For example, if your desire is to become more orgasmic, imagine the sensation of a longer, more intense orgasm—the sounds you make as you reach climax, the feel of the energy spreading through your body, and the smell of your sexual essences.

Form a statement that encapsulates your goal and captures the essence of your vision. It can be phrased as a statement of will—"My will is to have a better job" or "I want to become more orgasmic, "or reduced to a simple phrase—"better job" or "more orgasmic." So, the goal "I want more intimacy in my life" becomes "more intimacy." Write out the phrase in full. Then strike out any duplicated letters, so that "more intimacy" becomes "moreintacy." Some magicians also choose to remove vowels, as these are not written in the Hebrew alphabet.

When you have the reduced form of your phrase, combine the letters into an aesthetic glyph (see diagram below). It is usually easier to use capital letters. They can be turned upside down or sideways, elongated, or curved, and can share lines with other letters. Let your imagination go and have fun. Your concentrated intent as you work on your sigil is the first stage of charging it with energy.

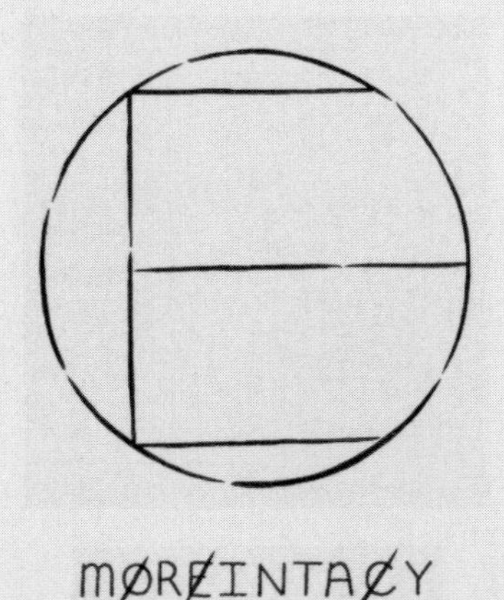

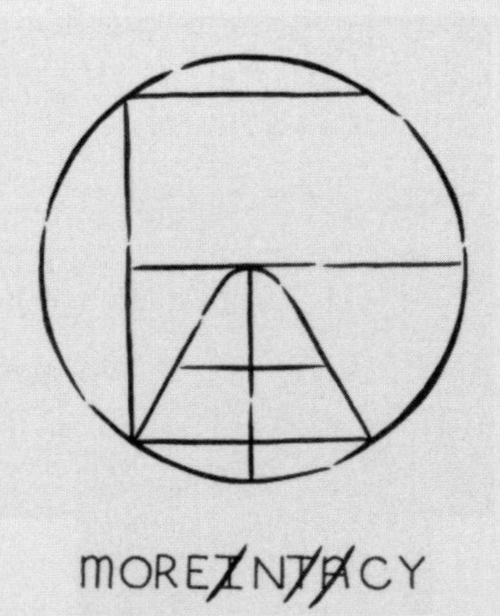

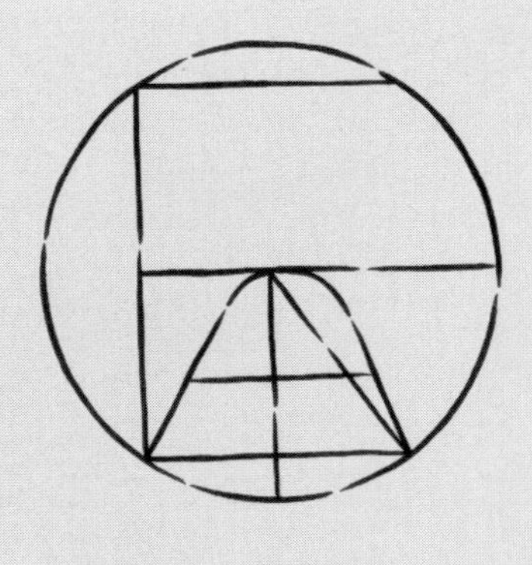

When you have finished creating your sigil, take a good look at it. Does your instinct tell you that you have correctly captured your vision in abstract form? If not, cancel that sigil by burning it and start again. If you feel happy and excited about your creation, then the next step is to imprint and charge it with energy.

Place your sigil somewhere comfortable to look at. Meditate upon it, casting an imprint of the symbol in your mind's eye. Take as much time as you need.

When you are ready, the sigil can be charged with sexual energy during a self-pleasuring ritual in your sacred space. At the moment of final orgasm, visualize your sigil. In Sex Magick rituals the physical sigil (the drawing on paper) is then anointed with spiritualized sexual fluids. Bury it in deep ground where it will not be discovered, then forget about it and let its magic work!

USING NUMBERS

Numbers can also be incorporated into sigils. This system, based on the Hebrew alphabet, where each letter also has a numerical value, comes from the writings of Aleister Crowley, and is familiar to most modern magicians.

A	*Aleph*	1
B	*Beth*	2
G	*Gimel*	3
D	*Dalet*	4
H/E	*Heh*	5
V/U	*Vau*	6
Z	*Zayin*	7
Ch	*Kheth*	8
T	*Teth*	9
Y/I/J	*Yodh*	10
K	*Kaph*	20 (in middle of word) 500 (at end of word)
L	*Lamed*	30
M	*Mem*	40 (in middle of word) 600 (at end of word)
N	*Nun*	50 (in middle of word) 700 (at end of word)
S	*Samekh*	60
O/Aa/Ng	*Ayin*	70
P	*Peh*	80 (in middle of word) 800 (at end of word)
Tz	*Tzaddi*	90 (in middle of word) 900 (at end of word)
Q	*Qoph*	100
R	*Resh*	200
S/Sh	*Shin*	300
T/Th	*Tau*	400

Assign the corresponding number to each of the letters in your magical word or phrase. Add them up and, if you reach double figures, add those two together to create a single-digit total.

Tuning in to Your Partner

Turn toward me your azure eyes that are rich with stars!
For the divine balm of one delightful glance,
I will lift the veils from love's most obscure pleasures,
And you shall drowse in endless dream!

CHARLES BAUDELAIRE

Discussing your goals and visions with your partner in order to create a shared symbol, then meditating together on that symbol, is an excellent way to tune in to each other mentally before sacred lovemaking. Connecting with each other on every level beforehand ensures that your minds are in a similar state of calm awareness and that you are in true flow with the vibrations of your subtle bodies.

As well as helping you and your partner to be in tune with each other during lovemaking, the following attunement exercises (on pages 82–3), if practiced over time, will increase your ability to hold each other in mind while apart from each other.

If you are in a long-term relationship, taking time to share simple moments together in this way can also help to rekindle those early, "falling in love" feelings of profound intimacy, when the simple act of holding hands or just being close to your lover was a magical experience.

SHARED SOLAR BREATH

This exercise, which can be done clothed or naked, brings you gently into harmony with each other through the alignment of your breath. As you relax into the process, you will develop greater awareness of the energy of the solar chakra.

- Lie flat on your backs next to each other, head to toes.

- Relax and take deep, long breaths. Feel the weight of your bodies sinking into the ground as you let go of tensions.

- Rest your right hand gently on each other's abdomen. Close your eyes and feel the breath of your beloved, through the steady rising and falling of your hand on their solar plexus.

- Synchronize your breathing and, after a while, you may feel so attuned to each other that you feel like one single organism.

EYE-GAZING

Eye-gazing is one of the simplest and most effective ways to tune in to each other. It also works as an excellent meditation, drawing you calmly and naturally into the moment, and into a deeper connection with your lover.

- Having removed glasses or contact lenses, lie side by side, or sit opposite each other, and look lovingly into each other's eyes with a soft gaze. Don't strain your eyes—it's fine to blink when necessary. Looking into both eyes can be difficult, so you might want to focus on the left or right eye, but try not to flick between the two.

- Keep the gaze deep and full, into your lover's soul. Breathe in unison to heighten the sense of connection.

Touching each part
of your body,
I also touch my body
and I realize we are One.

FROM THE SHRI CHAKRA YANTRA CEREMONY

MAKING CONNECTIONS

These exercises come from the Islamic Sufi tradition and can be done clothed or naked. They are the first steps to creating energy circuits between you and your lover.

Sit cross-legged opposite each other with knees touching. If this is uncomfortable, try stretching one leg out and bending the other comfortably, with your partner doing the same opposite you.

Both of you place your right palm on the other's heart chakra. Now place your left hand over their right hand on your own chest. Gaze into each other's eyes and breathe in harmony. Feel the love connection between you streaming out of your hearts and back in through your hands.

In the same position, touch your foreheads together. Close your eyes and enjoy the feeling of closeness and intimacy. Try complementary breathing—as you exhale, send your breath into your lover's third-eye chakra. Pause while your partner inhales it from their third eye and exhales it back to begin the cycle again.

Making the connection between the two of you with the fingertips of both hands touching can be fun, and connects you energetically. Either rest your fingertips lightly against each other's, or play with increasing the pressure on each of your lover's fingertips in turn.

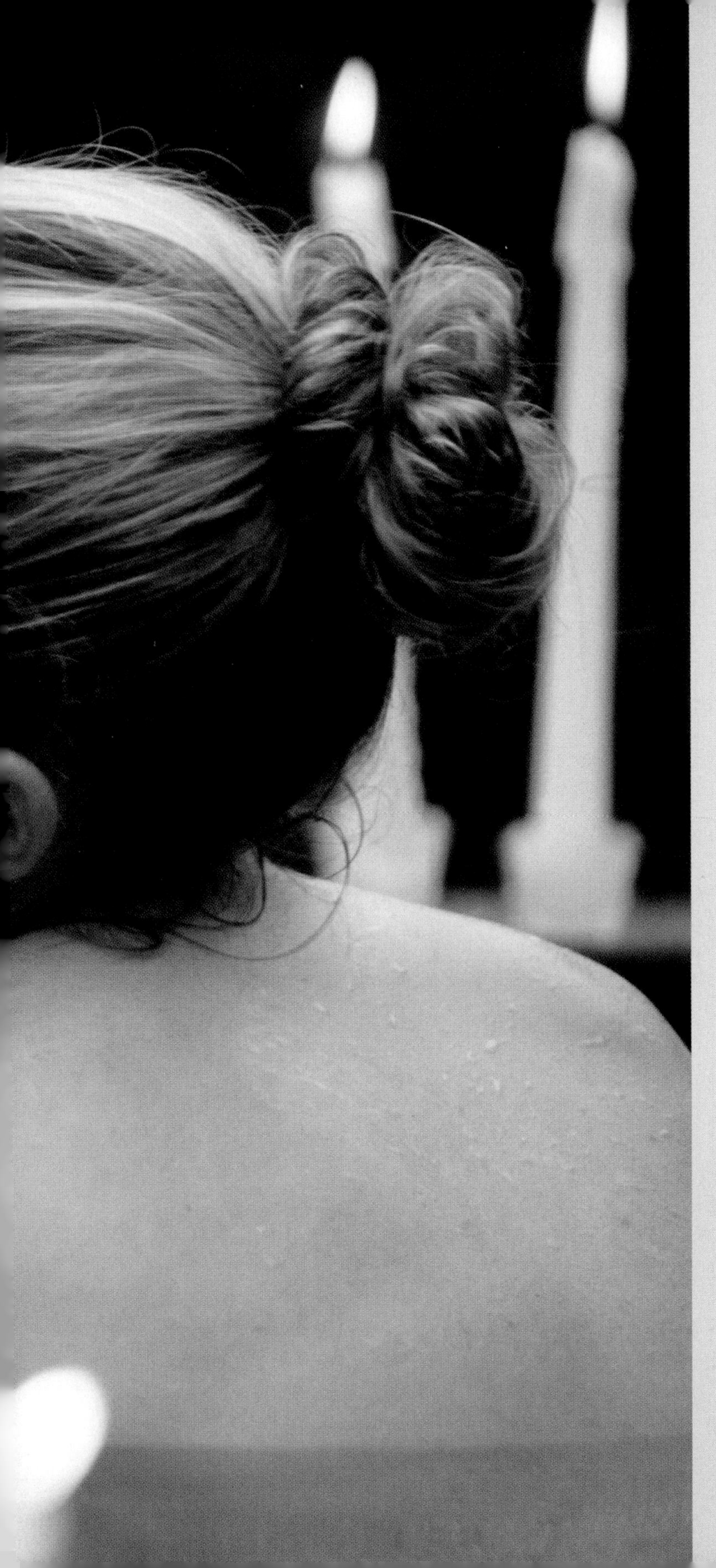

CHAPTER 4

Preparing a Sacred Space

A sacred space is an area that has been ritually cleansed and blessed for the purpose of meditation, spiritual work, and connecting with the divine. It is a physical space designed to enhance the sacred "space" within. Sacred spaces fulfil an instinctive human need to transform chaos into cosmos, and to create safe structures within which to explore extraordinary realities—from the simplicity of ceremonies around campfires to soaring Gothic cathedrals. They act as a bridge "between the worlds," allowing us to open ourselves to the divine.

In order to focus the mind and aid the harmonious flow of spirit during ecstatic lovemaking, you can create and bless your own personal sanctuary. This consecrated space will create order and stability; it will anchor you both as you tread the threshold between the known and the unknown, and protect you by keeping out harmful energies. It will itself be a profound act of creation.

SACRED SPACE VISUALIZATION

Take ten minutes to dream about your ideal sacred space. Let your imagination run wild and conjure up in your mind the perfect fantasy setting for sexual exploration and ecstasy. This visualization is fun and valuable to do as partnerwork if you have a regular partner who will be sharing the space.

Focus fully on every detail of your fantasy setting and include all the senses—how it would look and smell, what sounds there might be, natural or technological, the feel of the fabric and objects, and the taste of any ritual foods you might bring into it. It could be a large, airy room, bathed in sunlight from open doors leading out into a beautiful garden filled with the scent of roses and jasmine. It might be a huge, round bed, draped with sumptuous fabrics and lit by dozens of tiny candles, or a musky boudoir filled with soft cushions, singing bowls, and chimes. It could be out of doors, in a private cove—imagine the feeling of sand between your toes and the sound of the sea lapping against the shore, seagulls soaring and calling overhead. You can draw or write down in minute detail how this magical place looks.

Now ground your imaginings and think about how you might bring elements from your fantasy into reality and recreate it in your own home or garden. Fresh flowers and fruit could symbolize aspects of nature present in the garden. Pebbles from the beach or an indoor water feature could conjure up the sea, or rich velvet drapes may evoke an exotic setting.

If your partner is participating in the exercise, it is fascinating to discover how similar or different your dream havens might be. Combine your ideas in order to create the perfect space together, both in your imaginations and in reality.

Your sacred space is where you can find yourself again and again...

JOSEPH CAMPBELL

Creating Your Outer Temple

A sacred space is formed by two actions: the designing and creation of the space, and the blessing of it through ritual.

Your sacred space for sex does not have to be the bedroom. You might choose to dedicate another part of your environment and keep the bedroom for sleeping. Try consecrating a different area for the exploration of erotic spirituality. You can create a haven of sensuality by using a futon or cushions, soft rugs, and throws. Sectioning off an intimate space with screens and drapes works well, helping to convey the feeling of "space out of time," with a very particular purpose and atmosphere.

Natural settings that promote a sense of connection with the earth are ideal but not always practical. However, it is possible to recognize seasons and life cycles within your indoor temple with some thought. In Japanese homes one often finds an alcove, called a *tokanoma*, containing a scroll and a flower arrangement that is changed with the seasons to serve as a reminder that change is a natural and positive process. Fresh flowers, plants, and fruit can serve as substitutes for an outdoor setting. Shells, feathers, pebbles, and pieces of wood that you have collected can act as potent talismans to put you back in touch with nature.

Make sure you know north, south, east, and west from your space. Most spiritual paths associate the four cardinal directions with the four elements of the classical world. Generally, earth is linked to the north, air to the east, fire to the south, water to the west, and spirit is at the center.

Give thought to the shape of your space. Circles are a universal symbol of unity, and a representation of heaven and the universe that resonates on a very deep level. A circle is a boundary that protects and embraces, a holy enclosure—think of the "casting of a circle" used in pagan ceremonies, or the circular seating arrangement of a Native American sweatlodge. To soften the traditional square shape of a room you might cover hard corners with drapes and cushions, and form a circle around the bed area with stones, flowers, bowls of water, or (carefully used) candles.

Lighting should be soft and warm, for which candlelight is ideal. If your space is very small and fire a possible hazard, then think about using dimmer switches, colored lightbulbs (or gel filters on lights), shades that cast light in interesting directions, or colored scarves thrown over lamps. Don't forget to ensure that your temple is warm enough to allow you to be comfortably naked.

This is a place for the exercises
that will bring me
to where I want to be.

JOSEPH CAMPBELL

An altar reminds us of the sacred and of our relation to it. You might decide to make one by covering a low table, box, or shelf with a beautiful fabric and placing sacred objects, such as statues of deities, fresh flowers, or a picture on it. You could include something to represent each of the four elements—candles for fire, incense or a feather for air, a bowl of water, and a bowl of soil or a rock for earth.

Consider the positioning of your altar. In Buddhist households, for example, the Buddha image is always given the highest "seat" in the room. So, in the shrine-room, this will be on the highest part of the shrine. If it is placed on a special shelf (often carved and decorated with color and gold), then that shelf is usually high on the wall and has nothing above it. Practitioners of Wicca generally place their altar in the north of the room, or in the center of the room, with the back of the altar to the north.

A word of warning: beware of clutter. Each object on your altar, and in your sacred space generally, should have a clear meaning or use for you. Take the opportunity, every time you recreate your divine sanctuary, to look at each object afresh and to decide if it is beautiful and special enough to be there. If not, discard it.

Your outer temple can be as elaborate as your imagination allows, or as simple as a circle of stones by a stream in a secluded spot. What matters is that you have designated it as a personalized sacred space, somewhere in which you can connect with spirit, where your energy is allowed to flow, a space in which to be open to sexual ecstasy.

Design your temple so that it stimulates and delights all the senses, creating a joyful atmosphere. You might consider including some of the following elements:

Smell: Flowers, ideally scented, such as lilies or jasmine, freshly cut herbs, incense; oil burners with essential oils of rose, lavender, sandalwood, or ylang ylang.

Touch: Cushions and soft rugs; velvet throws; silk hangings; feathers.

Sight: Mirrors; crystals; prisms—hung in a window these can cast wonderful rainbows throughout the space; candles, floating in water for a beautifully diffused light; colors—red and yellow are traditionally favored for tantric work, but violet is also effective; symbols—yantras and mandalas, ideally those you have created yourself.

Sound: Wind chimes; water fountains; gongs; singing bowls; drum or didgeridoo; rainstick; a stereo, for appropriate music.

Taste: Offerings of fresh fruit; small squares of rich, dark chocolate; a ritual goblet of wine or juice on trays.

Left Krishna visiting his lover, Radha. Indian book illustration from the Punjab, c. 1685. The epic hero Krishna was an incarnation of the god Vishnu, the Preserver. His favorite gopi, or milkmaid, Radha, symbolizes the human soul.

Sacred Space Ritual

As much as our body
requires food for
nourishment,
our souls and spirit
require ritual to stay whole.

MALIDOMA PATRICE SOME

Why Ritual?

A ritual is an action performed with intention for a specific purpose. We use rituals to give everyday life significance, to provide form and guidance, and to mark transitions. Their use creates a context for our lives.

All of us perform unconscious rituals every day, from our domestic morning routines to the route we take home from work. We also participate consciously in social and cultural rituals, such as the formal rites of passage used to recognize major life transitions—baptisms, bar mitzvahs, weddings, funerals. These time-honored ceremonies can speak to us through the sheer weight of their history and their use of ancient symbols. Consciously self-created rituals, however, have the added power of self-expression, creativity, and highly personal meaning.

We also have our own very intimate rituals that we share with family, friends, and lovers—from the different ways in which we celebrate Christmas, Thanksgiving, or New Year, to the trip to the football game with friends every Saturday afternoon to support our team. Perhaps you and your lover mark certain occasions, such as anniversaries, with a meal in the restaurant in which you had your first date, or always make a point of ending phone calls with the words "I love you." In this way, ritual can provide a sense of stability, continuity, and reassurance in a rapidly changing world.

Conscious ritual can also be used to mark the passage from the profane to the sacred—such as the rite of blessing with holy water, and genuflection before taking a seat in a church—and to the start of sacred time, the time of rebirth and renewal. It is the cue to switch awareness into a different, deeper mode, consciously removing ourselves from our ordinary existence. It moves us toward the possibility of mystical experience, and the realm of myth and magick.

Rituals provide the opportunity for a time of stillness and focus, the chance to reconnect with our inner mind and selves, free from disturbance. They offer the potential for transformation and, by participating in them, we acknowledge ourselves as players in the world, rather than victims. The commitment to create change implicit in a ritual performed with specific intent is an act of empowerment.

When we create a sacred space, our rituals themselves become fields of energy. The very act of charging a space with sacred intent—whether by the swinging of a censer, the sprinkling of water, or the blowing of tobacco smoke as in Native American ritual—creates an energy form that keeps out negative energies and keeps in the energy and power created so that it can rise to a peak.

Full participation in ritual expands us,
calls forth and gives expression to
dormant parts of our nature:
artist, teacher, lover, healer, visionary,
shaman, wild-man or -woman, god or goddess.
A ritual performed in the sanctuary
of our sacred space is an initiation.
It empowers us to express
our wild, ecstatic, visionary selves.

MARGO ANAND

Preparing Your Outer Temple

Your sacred space should be prepared anew and recharged with ceremony each time it is to be used for the purpose of erotic union and connection. You are creating an alchemy of mood, blessing your outer temple to protect it, inviting in positive energies, and marking your sacred intention.

The act of preparation starts with clearing, cleansing, and purifying your space, and while this part might seem like a chore, it is itself a vital element of the ritual if approached with awareness, helping to establish focus for the time ahead. It is also part of treating your space as a temple—every spiritual tradition has cleansing and purification rites to sanctify its temples and sacred spaces.

Begin by clearing your space of clutter. Clutter is symbolic of energy that is stuck, and getting rid of it will make you feel lighter in mind and body. If your environment is full of rubbish and clutter your inner energy will reflect this—it will be slow and sluggish. By clearing your space you are welcoming in new, vibrant energy.

Now tidy, clean, and dust. Surprising as it may seem, cleaning with awareness can be a form of meditation. Notice the sensations as you sweep and dust. Observe your breathing, the feel of the air entering and leaving your nostrils, and how your breathing changes as you put more effort into your scrubbing or reach upward to remove a cobweb from an awkward corner.

In Zen Buddhism there is a story in which a student asks his master:

"Master, how do you put enlightenment into action? How do you practice it in everyday life?"

The master replies: "By eating and by sleeping."

Confused, the student says: "But everybody sleeps and everybody eats."

The Master answers: "But not everybody eats when they eat, and not everybody sleeps when they sleep."

It is the same with cleaning. Do it with your full attention, being present in the moment, consciously paying attention to the here and now, and it can become the essence of mindful practice. As you clean, be especially rigorous around the corners, and in nooks and crannies where stale energy tends to accumulate.

Freshen the air by opening windows and cleanse the space of negative energy. An effective way of doing this is by "smudging" the area with a wand of smoldering sage. Also known as "sweeping the smoke," this is a powerful method of purification often used before Native American rituals. Sage is traditionally burned as a protection against malevolent energies, and used to establish a sacred boundary at the start of a ceremony. It is a strong purifier and has the power to draw away any negative energies that may be stuck in an area. You could also try spraying, using water scented with your favorite essential oil. (Water sprayers for plants are particularly good for this function.) A traditional way to purify space is to sprinkle salt and water around the edges—as well as being effective cleansing materials they also help renew our connection with the earth and nature. As you smudge, spray, or sprinkle, remove negative energies by scooping with your hands and sending them out of an open window or door, or, afterward, sweeping them out with a besom broom, Wicca fashion.

These purifying actions are particularly effective when used in conjunction with sound. Intoning sacred words, such as the mantra "OM," can help to crystallize the energy in a space, or you could state your intention while you smudge, spray, or sprinkle. An example might be "May this space be filled with love and light."

Clapping, and ringing deep-sounding bells, are used in feng shui to clear energy. Start at the entrance of the space, then clap or ring in each corner, close to the wall. Begin with your hands above your head and continue clapping or ringing down the wall. Wash your hands afterward to rid yourself of any stale energy "stuck" to them.

When my beloved returns to the house,
I shall make my body into a Temple of
Gladness. Offering this body as an altar of
joy, my let-down hair will sweep it clean.
Then my beloved will consecrate this temple.

VAISNAV BAUL SONG

CORD OF POWER

Cords and knots are magical tools used in pagan rituals. Witches usually wear a cord around the waist during rituals, showing that they are bound to the Gods, the color often indicating their level of initiation or craft speciality.

In handfasting ceremonies (pagan and Celtic marriage rites), lovers are symbolically bound to each other by the hands to celebrate the binding nature of their love. During the ceremony, the couple face each other and, stretching out and crossing their arms, join left hands and right hands together. When viewed from above their arms and bodies form a figure eight—an ancient religious symbol for the union of man and woman. A cord is then tied loosely around their hands. A year and a day after being handfasted, they may return to the sacred circle and repeat their vows with the cord tightly knotted. This symbolizes their intention to have a permanent relationship and is the source of the expression "to tie the knot."

A Cord of Power may be used to protect your sacred space.

- Having measured the diameter of your room, buy a length of rope of about finger thickness, tie the two ends, then place it around the edge of your space so that it lies flat against the walls.

- Objects that represent the four quarters (see page 26) can be attached to the rope, to the east, south, west, and north. These could be a piece of topaz crystal, red jasper, turquoise, and a silver coin.

- The cord must then be consecrated with earth, water, fire, and air to provide protection in the four directions. Splash it with holy water, waft it with incense, sprinkle it with salt, and breathe on it nine times.

- Your cord of power should be placed in its own bag in a safe place when not being used.

Preparing Your Inner Temple

After preparing your outer temple, it is just as important to think about cleansing your inner temple—your body. Having a bath or shower before ecstatic lovemaking is not just a matter of hygiene, of washing the everyday grime and sweat from your body. It helps to mark the change in time and worlds. As the water runs over you in the shower, or drains down the plughole of the bath, you can feel your day-to-day thoughts and concerns running away with it, clearing away all the distractions, worries, and anxieties that can hamper concentration.

Sharing a bath with your lover can be a wonderful way to relax and set the scene for the intimacy to follow. Prepare the bathroom with incense and candles, use relaxing essential oils to scent the warm water, and make an occasion of it. If you are fortunate enough to have a large bath then bathe together, otherwise take turns to massage, soap, and rinse each other from head to toe.

After bathing, a period of quiet stillness, a short meditation, or a visualization, such as opening your chakras (see pages 58–9), can help to change your mindset at this point from the mundane to the sacred.

Think about what you will wear. You might decide to be naked or, if undressing each other is to be part of the

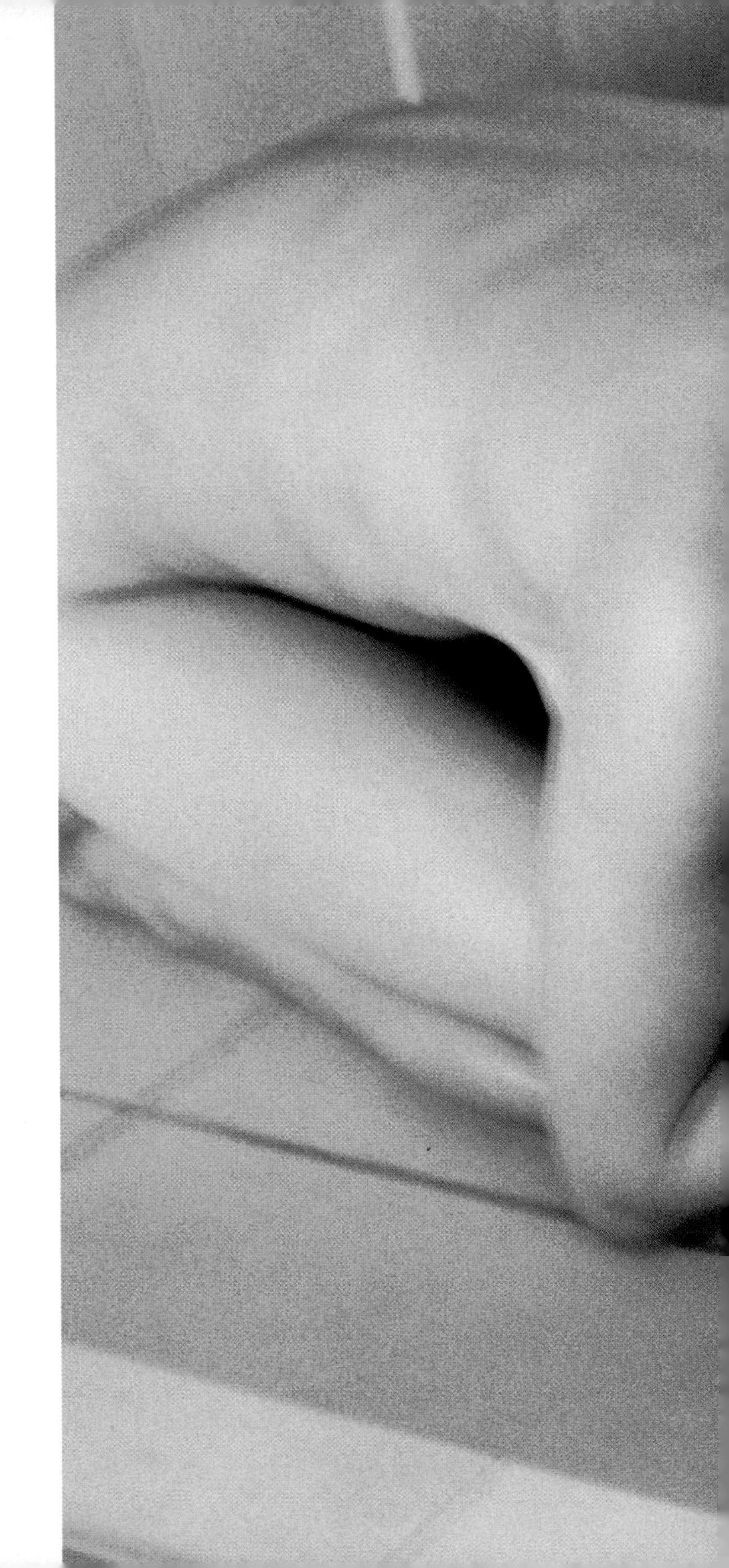

fun later on, put on special clothes or underwear made of sensuous fabrics. Whatever your choice of clothing (or none), make sure to take off your shoes and socks so that you are barefoot, with nothing between your feet and the ground on which you stand, walk, and dance. This act removes a layer of deadness and familiarity between you and the earth. You'll instantly feel more alive by divesting yourself of your shoes and socks—try it! Not for nothing did Moses hear a voice from the Burning Bush commanding him, "Take off your shoes! This is holy ground..."

Creating Your Ritual

To be effective, a ritual must be composed of actions, tools, and symbols that have inner meaning for you. It is not the mindless repetition of someone else's words—it is about what works and what has meaning for *you.* Your heart, mind, body, and soul have to be fully engaged—there is no point in simply going through the motions.

Every ritual is concerned with emotions and life, whether it's a social rite of passage, a blessing for your sacred space, or a rite you perform as you ride the waves of orgasmic bliss. The special ritual with which you initiate your own sacred sexual experience should always be personal and perfect for you.

Your ritual does not have to be long or complicated. It can be as simple as the act of lighting a candle, invoking a mood, or embracing your beloved. What matters is the quality of thought that has gone into creating the ceremony to make it as meaningful as possible.

Think deeply about the function of your ritual, and how best you can mark the transition to that special space and time in which you awaken yourself to the power and possibilities of erotic spirituality. Will you be using the space on your own, for self-exploration and pleasuring, or with a partner? If you are sharing your space, then you will want to create your ritual with your lover.

Openings and closings are very important, so plan ahead not only how you will start your ritual, but also how you will bring it to a clear and satisfying ending.

As you devise further rituals, consider the elements of continuity and change. Some parts of your ritual will be the same each time—perhaps the candle you burn or the music you play—while others, such as the invocation, may change according to your purpose.

Don't forget, a ritual is serious but it need not be solemn. Make it fun; make it a joy to perform. It is not a chore but a heartfelt thing of beauty that you have created to celebrate and mark the transition to the sacred.

Here are some suggestions for ritual that you could adapt to your own needs or use to spark off thoughts:

- ❖ Mark the beginning and end of the ritual in a clear way, with a full-body embrace with your partner, for example, or by ringing a bell or beating a drum.
- ❖ State your intention, keeping it as simple as possible. It could be broad—"We dedicate this space to joyful celebration of our connection with each other and with the divine"—or more specific to what you will be sharing.
- ❖ You might also want to invoke the qualities of celebration, experimentation, receptivity, and reverence.
- ❖ Call in the four directions to invoke a sense of connection with the cosmos—place four candles at the edges of your space, one in each of the four quarters or cardinal directions (see page 88), or ring bells at the four quarters.
- ❖ You could also recite a favorite or new-found love poem that encapsulates your intention.
- ❖ Think about incorporating periods of quiet into your ritual, perhaps through a meditation or visualization, and also sounds, such as drums, bells, or chanting.
- ❖ Raise your Kundalini energy with dancing, drumming, or singing—whoop and holler!
- ❖ Share a goblet of wine or juice with your lover.
- ❖ Choose a special piece of music or song that you play only on these occasions to create a particular mood. It could be uplifting, contemplative, soothing—whatever works for you, whether it is Bach, New Age ambient sounds, or modern dance music.

The Wicca teacher Starhawk suggests these excellent ways to visualize protection for your space:

- ❖ Think of a favorite color and imagine it as a ribbon of light enclosing your space.
- ❖ Imagine a time when you have felt safe and a place in which you have felt safe. Pick a color, sound, or image that reminds you of that place and imagine it encircling your space.

When your ritual is complete and your sacred space has been blessed, you can go ahead and practice sexual magic confident in the knowledge that you have created a safe and special place in which to open up and explore new realms, and that everything that takes place within it will be treated with love, respect, and trust.

Decorate the beautiful walls of the love-chamber with
pictures and other objects upon which the eye
may dwell with delight.
Scatter some musical instruments and refreshments,
rosewater, essences, fans and books containing
amorous songs and illustrations of love-postures.
Splendid wall lights should gleam, reflected by wide
mirrors, while both man and woman should not
have any reserve or false shame, giving themselves
up in complete nakedness to their unrestrained
passions, upon a fine bed, ornamented with many
useful pillows and covered with a canopy.
The sheets should be sprinkled with flowers and scent,
and sweet incense should be burned.
In such an environment let the man, ascending the
throne of love, enjoy the woman in ease and
comfort, gratifying both his and her
every wish and whim.

ANANGA RANGA

Right Beneath a curving canopy lovers embrace in the sitting position. The garlands of flowers they have exchanged are set aside. Rajput School, late eighteenth century.

CHAPTER 5

Building and Sharing Sexual Energy

In any sexual encounter, powerful and creative energy is aroused. You may have sensed this more strongly at certain moments during lovemaking than others, when you experience an intense feeling of closeness with your lover. This natural intercoursing of energies between sexual partners is the raw material that sexual mystics turn into spiritual gold. Sex-positive spiritual traditions regard the energy created and unified during sexual union as the key to uniting spirit with flesh, and so heaven with earth.

During the act of love, powerful energy circuits are activated. These circuits can also be developed independently, exchanged with your partner in non-sexual ways, and then consciously brought into your lovemaking to good effect. This chapter looks at exercises that will help you to become aware of your energy flow and raise it within your body, and shows you how to pass energy back and forth creatively with your lover.

Breath of Life

Modern science has shown us that what we once took to be the
material world is, when seen from another perspective,
in fact a manifestation of pure energy.
Our bodies depend upon having a source of energy (food) to function.
We are bombarded with energy from the Sun
and from other sources in our environment.
As earthly creatures, we are energetic beings.
And nowhere is this shown more than in our sexual lives.

WALT WHITMAN, *I SING THE BODY ELECTRIC*

Breath is life. At its most basic, if you don't breathe you die. But how we breathe also affects how we live; it has a profound impact on our energy, awareness, and consciousness. An understanding of the power of breath is essential for working with sexual energy. Most of us do not breathe naturally—stress, sedentary lifestyles, and muscular tension lead us to take short, quick, and shallow breaths, depriving our bodies of oxygen. We seem to have forgotten how to breathe naturally, with our whole bodies rather than just the upper chest, and studies show that we use only a small proportion of our total lung capacity.

In stressful situations we tend to tense up and, without even realizing it, our breathing becomes more shallow. Similarly, when approaching orgasm, it is common to hold the breath, which stops the flow of sexual and creative energy—exactly the opposite of what we are trying to achieve with sacred sex.

In contrast, being in tune with our breathing leads to a meditative state of conscious awareness. In sacred sexual union the aim is to realize full breathing, so as to absorb and channel your sexual energy. You learn to use breath consciously during sex to alter your levels of arousal,

enhance the connection between you and your lover, and to channel energy. Breath is power, and deep-breathing exercises are a means of harnessing that power.

In Tantric sex, breath control, *pranayama*, is used to move and store *prana*, the life force in the body. Tantrics believe that our state of mind is closely linked to the quality of *prana* in our bodies. As breath control influences the flow of *prana*, so we can influence our state of mind through the quality of our breath.

Taoism, too, has a breathing science, called *chi gung*, which focuses on breathwork based on a balance of Yin and Yang. Through breath we draw on the cosmic power of the universe, and Taoists believe that correct breathing enhances our store of *chi*, or vital energy, and also drives and distributes *chi* through the body's invisible network of energy meridians. Taoists traditionally believe that each person has a finite number of breaths in their life, so it makes sense to learn to breathe more deeply and slowly to lengthen our time here—every breath and heartbeat saved now prolongs life later.

The holiness of breath is not limited to the Eastern traditions. The creation story in the Bible tells that humans were created when God breathed his divine breath into the clay. The mystical Jewish *Zohar* teaches that the union between God and humanity occurs through the medium of the breath. The Christian mystic Hildegard of Bingen defined prayer as breathing in and breathing out the one-breath, or spirit, of God.

Types of Breathing

The following exercises aim to move us away from the idea of breath as a simple, automatic function of the nervous system; instead they enable us to work with it as a powerful transformational tool to create unity of mind and body.

There are four main types of breathing that can be used during sex to produce varied and wonderful effects:

❖ Deep and slow breathing is the cornerstone breath of conscious sex. It promotes a calm and meditative state of mind, and can have a cooling-down effect. For this reason, it is one of the key tools with which to delay ejaculation or orgasm. Shared rhythmic deep breathing when approaching orgasm can also intensify the emotions and sensations, bringing them to an incredible pitch.

❖ There is also a place for fast and hard breathing, which can have a purifying effect. This is a "heating-up" breath that energizes and arouses, and can be quite forceful. The "breath of fire" is a fairly extreme example of this kind of "strong" breathing, but simply panting rapidly from your stomach, with an open mouth, is also useful as a quick "heat-up," and is a good antidote to the tendency to hold the breath when reaching heightened states of arousal. Energizing breathing intensifies emotions, aids with strenuous physical movement, and can be used to increase levels of arousal and intensify orgasm.

Sharing breathing is a profoundly intimate form of non-verbal communication, and there are two forms this can take:

❖ Synchronous breathing is breathing in tune with your lover. You both inhale together and exhale together. This type of breathing may decrease arousal, but it enhances the sense of intimacy and connection with your partner and also provides a very peaceful rhythm to your lovemaking. Synchronous breathing is great for sharing energy-moving visualizations together.

❖ The opposite of synchronous breathing is complementary breathing. In this type of breath, as one partner exhales, the other inhales, and so on, in a kind of circular pattern. Complementary breathing can increase arousal and strengthen polarity. It also enables powerful energy circulation to take place if visualizations are added.

Exercises to help you develop each of these types of breathing are outlined in the following overleaf, but before trying any of them, take the time to sit quietly and calmly and become aware of your breath. Sit comfortably with both feet firmly on the ground, a straight spine, and your shoulders relaxed, or lie flat on the floor with head, neck, and spine in a straight line. Breathe normally through your nose and focus on the passage of air through your body as you inhale and exhale completely. Warm your hands and place them just under your ribs. Feel the rise and fall of your diaphragm as the breath comes and goes from your lungs. As you take smooth, slow breaths try to "watch" your breath and still your mind. Experience how your body and mind feel different with full breaths compared with when you are breathing quickly and less deeply.

Don't force your breath. Work slowly and gently. Trying too hard will simply cause your muscles to tense, making it even harder to take full and calm breaths. If you are having trouble with a technique, resist the temptation to "push" the breath and instead relax, warm your hands, place them on your stomach, and give yourself a gentle massage to ease the muscles and focus your awareness.

After completing these exercises sit quietly for a few moments and feel their effect on your body and mind.

SOLO BREATHING EXERCISES

Through conscious, rather than automatic, breathing you can improve your quality of life by changing your state of mind. These exercises demonstrate the healing, cleansing, and rejuvenating power of the breath.

Complete Breath

For this exercise, you will need to sit down on the floor, cross-legged, or lie down on your back in a relaxing, comfortable position. Keep your eyes and mouth closed, breathing through your nose.

Blow out all the air in your abdomen through your nose, then inhale deeply. Imagine the air being pulled upward toward your abdomen, then up into the rib cage, upper lungs, chest, and throat.

Retain the breath here, keeping your face and body relaxed. Don't tense up with the effort and only hold your breath for as long as is comfortable—the aim is not to get light-headed or pass out.

Exhale slowly, pushing the air out from throat, chest, rib cage, then abdomen. Pause before inhaling for the next round.

Keep all three parts of your breath—inhalation, retention, and exhalation—the same length. As you practice, allow the length of the inhalation, retention, and exhalation to increase, but never beyond the point of comfort.

Healing Breath

This is a simple extension of the complete breath. Whereas in the complete breath the time spent on the inhalation, retention, and exhalation was equal, here the ratio is consciously altered so that the breath is held for four times as long as the inhalation, and the exhalation takes twice as long as the inhalation. For example, if you inhale for a count of four, you will hold for sixteen, then exhale for eight. Once again, the retention of the breath should not create any discomfort that would make you tense up.

Start off gently and you will find that, with practice, you can increase the length of time for which you can hold your breath.

While retaining your breath, feel and appreciate the absolute stillness and sense of calm in body and mind.

Don't consciously count the length of each part of this breathing exercise, or try to measure it with a clock. Instead, just feel it by becoming aware of the rhythm of your body—your heartbeat, pulse, and the sound and sensation of each element of the exercise (inhalation, retention, and exhalation).

Alternate Nostril Breathing

This exercise can look and feel odd, but it is wonderful for clearing any blockages to air flow in the nostrils and re-establishing the natural nasal cycle (we naturally alternate our breathing, at roughly two-hour intervals in a healthy person, between the two nostrils throughout the day). This exercise cleans and rejuvenates the vital channels of energy of the subtle body and balances the left and right sides of the brain.

Sit comfortably with your back straight. Take a couple of deep, complete breaths, then lift your right hand to your face and press and close the right nostril with the thumb of your right hand. Draw in a deep breath through the left nostril.

Focus on the energy you are breathing in and, after taking a full breath, close your left nostril by holding the third and fourth fingers of your right hand lightly against it, and hold your breath. While you are doing this, make sure your face and mouth remain relaxed and don't tense up.

Taking your thumb away from your right nostril, slowly exhale, making sure you expel the breath fully. Now inhale through your right nostril. After a full inhalation, close your right nostril with your thumb and retain the breath again before releasing the fingers from your left nostril. Breathe out through your left nostril. This is one round. The ratio of time spent on the inhalation-retention-exhalation can be 1:1:1 or 1:4:2. Start by trying to do five rounds and gradually build up the number of inhalations and exhalations.

Do not force the breath through your nostrils as you exhale in this exercise; make sure your breathing is gentle and natural. Don't attempt alternate nostril breathing if you have a cold or blocked nasal passages.

Breath of Fire

This is a warming, purifying breath powered by abdominal contractions. The breath is localized in the solar plexus chakra and stimulates Kundalini, charges the nervous system, and clears the mind. Air is pulled in and pumped out rhythmically while the abdominal muscles, chest, rib cage, and shoulders remain relaxed.

Start with a session of long, deep breathing; then, once the lungs are fully expanded, contract your abdominal muscles upward tightly to push the air out—you should hear a "whoosh" or "huh" sound. Then relax the abdominal muscles, allowing them to drop. Air is drawn into the lungs as you do so.

With each breath, contract and relax faster until you feel a rhythm. Allow that rhythm to take over. Finish this exercise with more long, deep breaths.

SHARED BREATHING EXERCISES

In these shared breathing patterns, you and your lover are taking a journey together, floating on your breath connection to a place of profound intimacy and peace. Yet tuning in to each other's breath, and learning to match or complement it, is such a simple act that it is ideal for trying with a new partner or with a long-standing lover who might not yet be completely at ease with the idea of incorporating ecstatic practices into your love life.

Synchronized Breathing

Sit facing your partner and establish an eye-gazing connection (see page 82).

Decide which of you will set the pace by breathing in a slow, gentle rhythm. The other matches their breathing so that you both inhale and exhale at the same time.

The active partner (the one who sets the pace) might need to adjust the speed of their breathing so that you can both establish and maintain a natural rhythm.

Once this is achieved you can add a visualization, drawing the energy upward from your base chakras together. Raise the breath to each chakra in turn until you reach the crown.

Complementary Breathing

Complementary breathing can be a powerfully intimate experience. Some Tantric texts even describe it as a "binding breath" in which lovers absorb the life-force of their partner, and bestow their own, with each breath.

Again, sit facing each other and decide which of you will set the breathing pace. The chosen person then takes a complete breath, and the other begins to breathe in reverse—as one of you inhales, the other exhales.

In this exercise, too, you can use a visualization to help you circulate and increase energy: the active partner inhales, as it were, through the base chakra, and exhales through the heart center, while the receptive partner then inhales that breath in through the heart and exhales it out through the base chakra, so that a circuit of erotic energy is created between you.

Once you have mastered this, try breathing in different rhythms while maintaining the harmony between you, and alternate who begins and who follows.

Raising Energy

Sexual arousal is normally focused in one particular area—the genital and pelvic region. As we know, this can be a powerful sensation, but in sacred sex we are seeking something much greater and more fulfilling.

The process of transforming sex into a whole-body sensual and sacred experience brings more than just the genitals into bed. Genitally focused sex has as its goal a short and intense orgasm. The entire sexual experience is geared toward this end, and once it has been achieved the sexual energy is spent, never having moved beyond the root chakra. This kind of sex is a bit like trying to scratch a hard-to-reach itch—it is only temporarily satisfying.

In contrast, spiritual sex is about letting go of goals—it is like going on a journey without an end in sight. By transforming the sexual experience from a goal-oriented process into a series of moments of pleasure in the "now," we release the flow of sexual energy, and making love becomes a voyage of discovery, connection, and growth.

This does not mean that spiritual sex is not orgasmic. Quite the opposite! Learning to raise and direct sexual energy upward and throughout the body gives you the capacity to diffuse that energy so that the orgasm, rather than being isolated in one part of your anatomy, can rise up in waves of pure ecstasy throughout your whole body.

When the mounting excitement is
accepted rather than grasped,
it becomes a full realization of
spontaneity and the resulting orgasm
is not its sudden end but the
bursting in upon us of peace.

ALAN WATTS

The key to spiritual sex is to be able to feel relaxed in states of high arousal, and to work on ridding ourselves of the muscular tensions that can block the flow of energy. Allowing your energy to move freely in the pelvis, and then beyond, opens up the body to the pleasure its totality can provide.

By tuning our awareness through breath and movement, we can relax into the sensation of energy streaming through our bodies, rather than tense up and restrict it to a single area, which is what tends to happen in the "normal" orgasmic state. The following exercises allow you to get used to the feeling of energy flow and, by integrating breath and movement, to develop your ability to charge your body with energy and then move it around easily during lovemaking, thus opening up your body to its full orgasmic response.

RAISING SEXUAL ENERGY WITH PELVIC ROCKING

This exercise works directly on the base chakra, combining breath and movement to raise energy, awaken the subtle body, and open all the chakras. It releases tension in every part of your body and brings awareness to areas where energy may be blocked.

Stand with a straight spine, your feet firmly on the ground, about shoulder width apart, and knees slightly bent. Ideally your eyes should be closed, but if you have difficulty keeping your balance with them shut, keep them open, directing your gaze to the tip of your nose instead.

Take a few long, deep breaths, making sure to release any tension in your body and bring calm to your mind. Take another deep breath in and out.

Now, this time as you inhale, tuck in your pelvis and squeeze your love muscle (see page 40). Try not to tense your abdomen as you contract your love muscle.

Exhale through your mouth and release the contraction of the love muscle so that it swings backward slightly, to the position it was in before it was contracted.

Continue the inhale-tuck-squeeze and exhale-swing back-release pattern until you reach a comfortable rhythm, with each rock or swing and squeeze or release matching the length of the inhalation or exhalation. You should start to feel a stirring sensation around your pelvic region.

As you become accustomed to the tingling sensation, feel the flow of erotic energy rising in your pelvis and beginning to move upward along your spine. Start to visualize your chakras and become aware of the energy filling your first chakra, located at the base of the spine, with bright light.

As you breathe, rock, and squeeze, the energy gradually expands and spins until it fills the first chakra and moves up to the sacral chakra. It continues to rise with the rhythm of your breath and movement, lighting up the solar chakra in your navel, like a glowing, dancing fire. Upward it goes, spreading out to fill the whole of your chest, spiralling around the heart chakra.

Feel the warm energy created by your rocking, squeezing, and breathing circulating around your body, from your root chakra to pelvis, navel, and heart, and then up into your throat and third eye. As the energy expands and rises up to your crown it cascades out and down.

KUNDALINI SHAKING

Bathe in the glow of the sparkling sexual energy that is surrounding your body—you may well feel a trembling, almost orgasmic sensation throughout your entire body, and even beyond. This is because your subtle body is awakened and has been charged with the powerful energy you have raised.

Let go and relax into the warm glow, before beginning to draw the energy back in and downward, when you feel ready. Gradually close off all your chakras except the crown and root chakras.

Be patient with yourself if this exercise seems difficult to begin with—it is quite normal to have trouble with coordinating your breath and body. You are also unlikely to feel the full effects first time round, but it is an exercise that will repay the effort of regular practice.

This exercise is an adaptation of a dynamic meditation taught by the Indian mystic Osho. It is a wonderful way to charge your body with energy, relax tension blocks, and open yourself up to orgasmic response.

Prepare yourself by putting on some music that you know makes you want to move, ideally with a strong beat, and make sure that you have plenty of room to move around in.

Stand upright with your eyes closed. With both feet firmly on the ground and keeping your back straight and your tailbone tucked in (don't stick your bottom out, or push your pelvis forward), bend your knees as far as feels comfortable. Relax the rest of your body—you might find that your shoulders hunch up, so consciously lower them—and check for tension in your face and mouth, directing your mind and breath to those areas to relax them if necessary.

Take deep, full breaths in through your nose and out through your mouth. You will start to feel tremors of energy in your calves and thighs. Move your awareness to those sensations and try to merge into the trembling feeling, rather than tensing up.

As the tremors begin to expand through your legs, start to rock gently backward and forward from your feet. Feel the tremors move upward, expanding into your pelvis and hips. Be loose and let your whole body shake, feeling the energies moving up from your feet. Let go everywhere and become the shaking.

Now, dance yourself awake!

KUNDALINI SHAKING (CONT)

When such as I
cast out remorse
So great a sweetness
flows into the breast
That I must dance
and I must sing
For I am blessed by
everything.
Everything I look
upon is blessed.

W.B. YEATS

Breathe in a deep, long, circular flow, and tune in to the rhythm of your breath as you transform the shaking into fluid movements. Allow your body to expand and open as you direct your breath into any areas of tension or pain. Let your head, neck, shoulders, chest, hips, pelvis, legs, knees, and feet all release into the music as body, breath, and mind become one.

Visualize a bright current of light entering your body from the ground beneath and feel yourself become part of the eternal dance of life, of Shiva and Shakti, of Yin and Yang, becoming whole as body and mind merge. Awaken your chakras through your dance. Try earthy foot-stomping to stimulate your root chakra, hip-circling for the sacral chakra, and belly rolls for your solar plexus. Open up your heart, stretching out, and raise your arms above your head to embody the element of air as you reach your throat chakra.

Let whatever sounds emerge occur naturally—whoop, sing, scream, and sigh. Let yourself go as you sway, swirl, and shake the energy all around your body like a Sufi whirling dervish, dancing into a trance state as your whole body moves with the rhythm.

Dance wildly, feeling the beat of the music within your body with your heartbeat, surrendering to the beat of your inner pulse, and letting your body vibrate in tune with the universal life force.

When you reach the end of your whirling, drop to the floor and lie quietly. Listen to your body in the sudden stillness—to your breath, heart, and pulse beat, to the sound of the energy you have raised still swirling around you. Feel your body sinking into the ground beneath you, the gentle pull of gravity earthing your body and gradually returning you to the everyday world in a relaxed and energized state.

Working Together

Consciously working with the energy you raise with your partner during lovemaking is one of the most exciting aspects of sacred sex. Different postures are used to create biomagnetic circuits that channel the energy around and between your connected bodies, and these are described in more detail in Chapter Seven. However, it is the mind that is the key to fulfilling energy work, and we do not need to be physically united, or even naked, to experience the intimacy of shared energy flows.

Creating simple energy circuits with your lover while not engaged in sexual union has a number of benefits. If you have never consciously worked with shared energy before, these exercises offer a startling demonstration of the power of the energy you can create between you—while fully clothed! You will feel a profound sense of togetherness as you explore your connection with each other on a subtle, energetic plane.

In addition, to enable you to keep the energy flowing and directed while in different sexual positions and degrees of arousal, it can be helpful to practice initially without those heightened sensations. In this way you can grow accustomed to the sensation of energy-sharing, and so integrate it more naturally into your lovemaking.

CREATING ENERGY CIRCUITS

The following exercises, which can be combined with different types of breathing, form the basis of the energy circuits you will create during lovemaking.

Solo Handrubbing

This is a simple but highly effective exercise for developing awareness of your body's energy. It can be practiced solo to begin with, so that you can build up a good, tangible sense of the power of the energy within you.

Make sure you are sitting comfortably. Close your eyes, then rub your hands together quickly until they feel quite warm. Now move them away from each other, to a distance of about six to eight inches—you should be able to feel the flow of energy across the gap.

Feel what happens if you move your hands closer together (but do not allow them to touch) and further apart—you may feel increased resistance as you bring them closer to each other, until it almost feels difficult to bring them together, like the opposing poles of magnets.

Paired Handrubbing

This exercise helps to establish a rapport with your partner, enabling you to move energy together in a fairly simple way.

Sit opposite each other, with knees touching, and establish a strong eye-gazing connection. Both of you should rub your hands together vigorously, building up a good charge of energy. Now quickly put your hands out so that your palms face those of your partner, close but not quite touching. Feel the energy flowing between you. Try moving your hands closer together and further apart and sense the energy moving. Allow the energy to flow between you.

Palm Touching

In this exercise, the focus is on directing the movement of energy throughout the whole body as you and your partner create a flowing circuit together.

Sit facing your partner and establish eye-gazing contact with each other. With your arms out in front of you and parallel to the floor, turn your right palm face down, toward the floor, and left palm face up, toward the ceiling. With your partner's hands in the same position, press your palms together.

Now start to visualize the energy flow between you. Direct the energy flowing down your right arm, through your right palm and into your partner's left hand. As your partner does the same, you should feel energy entering your left palm from their right. Visualize that energy traveling up your left arm, across your shoulders and down your right arm, then through your right palm and back into your partner's left. You are creating a circuit of energy between you, by giving, receiving, and sharing energy.

Polarized Circulation

This exercise can be done naked and with sexual contact, but ideally it should be practiced clothed initially so that you can both concentrate fully on the simple circulation of energy at this stage.

Sit in the yab-yum position: one partner sitting cross-legged or in the lotus position, if they are capable, while the other sits in their lap, so they are face-to-face, with legs wrapped around their partner's hips.

Establish an eye-gazing rapport and complementary breathing. The partner at the bottom position inhales and visualizes the energy entering their body through their mouth, nose, eyes, and ears and then moving down the body. As they exhale, they direct the energy leaving their body through the genitals.

The partner on top inhales and directs the energy entering their body through their genitals upward. As the energy rises it increases in intensity and then exits through the mouth, nose, eyes, and ears as they exhale. Continue the cycle. A very powerful circulation of energy is being created that increases in power and intensity as the cycle goes round. Continue this exercise for as long as feels comfortable.

Circle of Psychic Protection

Nyasa is a Tantric ritual in which you form a mystic circle of protection around yourself and your beloved. *Nyasa* means "placing" and, through the concentration of consciousness on various parts of the body, openings are "sealed" to provide protection from negative energies outside and loss of energy from within. An erotic, polarized energetic circuit is created between you that opens the heart center and enhances intimacy.

Sit naked, opposite each other, and hold hands. Meditate together for a short time, attuning your minds to each other and synchronizing your breathing. Now, with a gentle touch of the fingertips, touch each other simultaneously on the palms, feet, genitals, navel, breasts, lips, ear lobes, eyelids, and third eye. You can start at the head and move down to the feet, or vice versa.

Repeating a mantra as you anoint each area can aid concentration—try "OM" or your own protective affirmation. In addition to touching, you could try breathing softly or placing a gentle kiss on each of the areas.

You are now protected as you explore the realms of sacred sex together with open hearts and calm minds.

Grounding Your Energy

Learning how to ground your energy is as important as being able to raise and direct it; when you are grounded you are brought to rest, solid and still, as one integrated flow of energy. Grounding is especially important if you find yourself feeling light-headed or out of control during any of the exercises, or if the energy starts to feel somewhat too chaotic. Taking a few full, deep breaths is a good place to start, followed by moving your energy into your feet, as making contact with the earth is nearly always a good way to center yourself physically and psychologically.

One of the simplest ways to reawaken your connection with the earth is to stamp your feet, first one then the other, establishing good contact with the solidity of the ground beneath you. Another easy grounding exercise is to rise up on your toes, from a standing position, then lower your heels to the ground (bending your knees as you do so), feeling yourself push against gravity then sinking into it. Making contact with the earth with both feet and hands is also very effective—stand solidly, with toes spread out to achieve the fullest contact with the ground, then bend down from the waist and, bending your knees as much as necessary, place your palms firmly on the ground with your fingers spread as far apart as comfortable. Push down with your hands and feet and take a few deep breaths.

It is a good idea to ground yourself after a particularly mind-blowing session of lovemaking. Taking a shower or eating something are two simple but effective ways of doing this. These activities can be shared with your lover to maintain the sense of intimate connection between you, while at the same time "earthing" you both so that you are ready to face the world again.

A GROUNDING MEDITATION

This meditation uses visualization to help you return to your body and find your connection with the earth. It can be done whenever you feel too much "in your head".

- Sitting in a chair, with your spine straight and both feet firmly on the floor, breathe deeply and regularly. Feel the solidity of the contact between your feet and the ground.

- Feel the weight of your body and the pull of gravity and visualize a strong column of light running between your body and the center of the Earth.

- Alternatively, imagine your body as a tree. Feel the roots extending down from your feet deep into the ground, pulling you into the earth. See your body as a solid trunk, holding firm against the push and pull of the energy around you. Breathe deeply and slowly into your roots and visualize them spreading out underground, holding you in the earth. Continue this meditation until you feel back in your body fully.

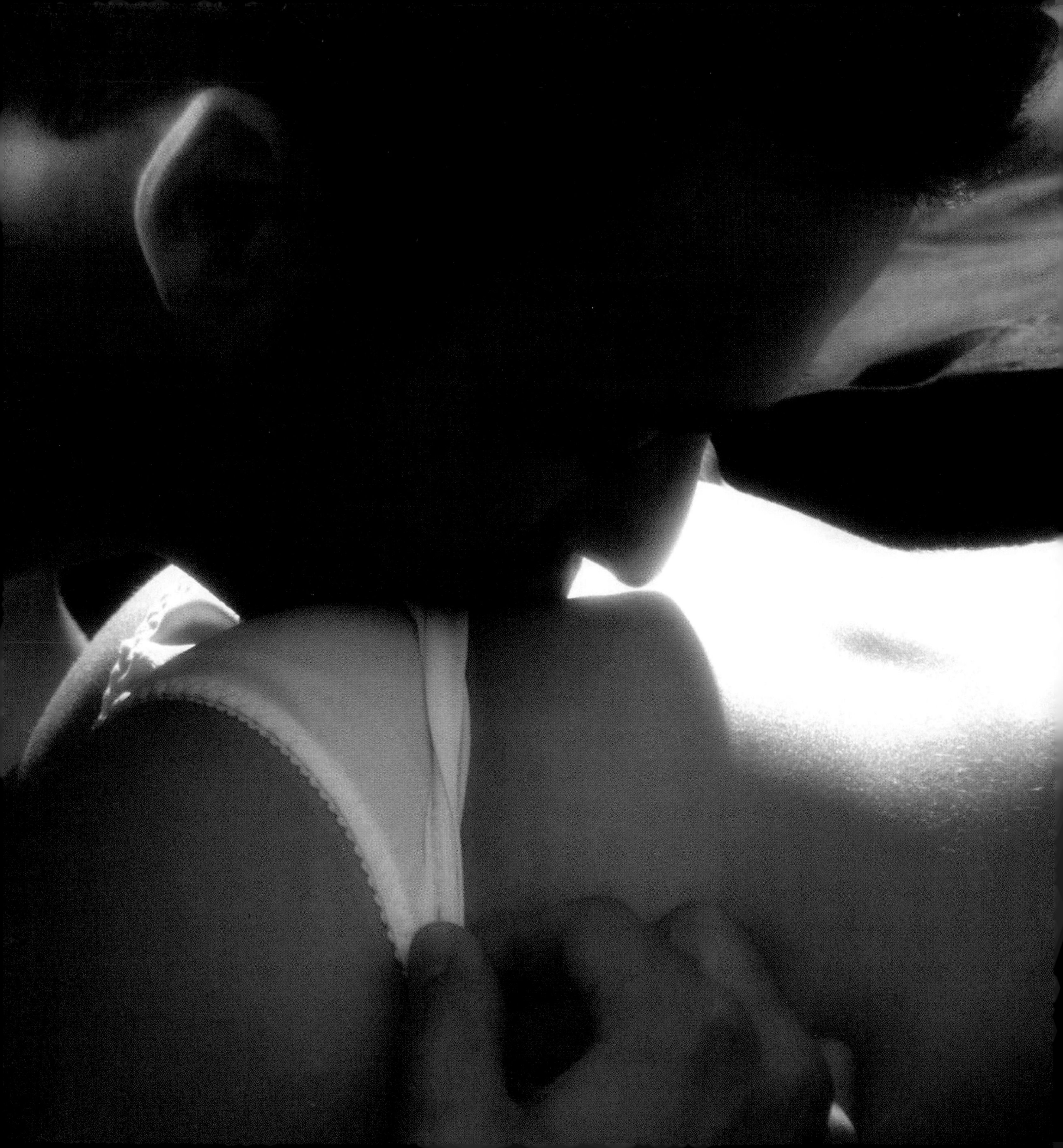

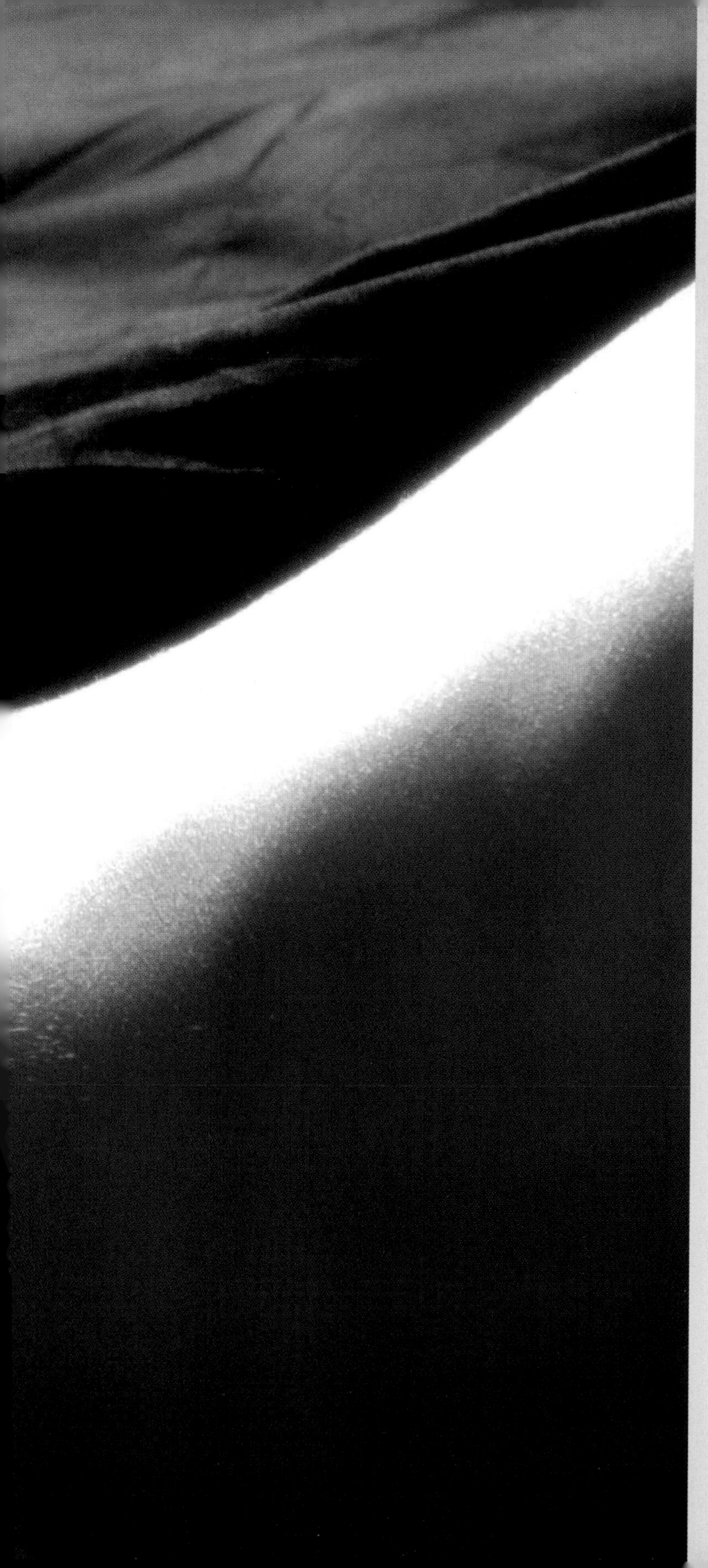

CHAPTER 6

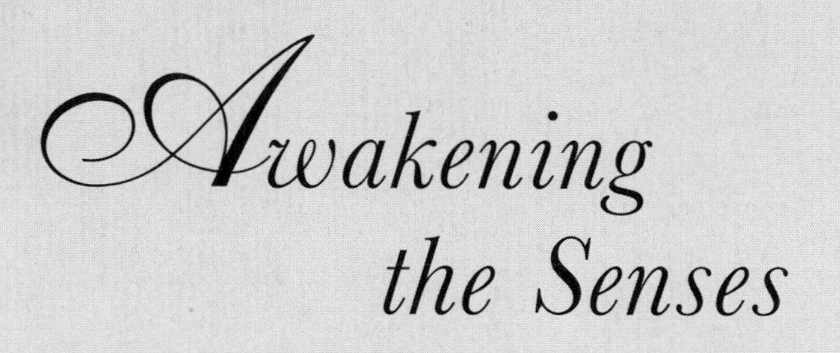

Awakening the Senses

Awakening the senses encompasses far more than is generally understood by the term "foreplay." In the journey toward sacred sexuality, awakening and arousal begins before you even touch each other, and goes on to involve all of the body and mind.

The journey starts with honoring the divine within, enabling you to meet and connect with your lover on a spiritual level, and to recognize the god and goddess energies within you both. Worshiping the divine nature of your lover is a sensual experience, as you explore each other's body with a tantalizing touch, discover erogenous zones, and harmonize your energies with sensual massage. Yoni and lingam worship are sacred and intimate acts that arouse sexual energy and create waves of erotic bliss as that energy moves throughout the body. Games to excite the senses also awaken playfulness and humor—essential elements in any sexual relationship.

Worshiping the Divine Within

You have the eyes of Hera,
the hands of Athena,
the breasts of Aphrodite.
Blessed is the man who looks upon you.
Thrice blessed is the man who hears you talk.
A demi-god is the man who kisses you.
A god is the man who takes you into bed.

RUTINOS

To move sexual energy into the sacred realm it is necessary to honor and awaken the spiritual power within yourself and your partner. By treating your body, and that of your lover, as a temple, love becomes an act of worship in which you reconnect with your own true nature. This process requires you to surrender to your own divine potential, and to invoke a sense of the divine within your partner.

When you take the time to recognize and appreciate the spiritual nature of your partner, it creates a more loving connection between you that has a resonance far beyond the hours you spend together making love. It extends into all facets of your relationship, how you hold each other in mind when apart as well as together, and forms a new context within which to deal with everyday petty squabbles and differences of opinion.

In Hindu Tantra, as we have seen, the human act of love mirrors the divine coupling of Shakti and Shiva, whose cosmic dance harmonizes the eternal forces of male and female. Men and women share in this divinity and are honored as earthly manifestations of these principles.

Tantrics therefore seek to make love literally as the god and goddess, calling them into their lovemaking through dressing-up, dancing, and meditation, aiming to make them manifest through posture, breath, and expression. With greater awareness of goddess energy, human sexual union becomes part of the eternal cosmic dance.

However you choose to envision the spiritual energies within, whether as literal or subtle manifestations of the eternal energy forces, by acknowledging, accepting, and embracing those forces you will connect with your partner on that divine level. Exploring and touching each other then becomes an act of mutual devotion and honoring.

Worship rituals help to focus the mind and enhance our internal feelings of devotion. Known as *puja* in Hinduism, devotional rituals dedicated to gods and goddesses are common in India's temples. Traditionally, in this form of worship the giver symbolically offers up an entire sensual world in order to be transformed. These rituals can easily be adapted and centered on your partner; to bring all the senses alive in your worship you might include bathing, feet-washing, giving gifts of flowers, ringing bells or chimes, lighting candles, or burning incense.

A simple ritual to honor the divine within will mark the beginning of your time together, helping you to tune in to each other, let go of lingering resentments, and renew the sense of sacred connection between you.

Left Krishna and Radha gaze at each other on a painted doorway in Rajasthan.

EYE-GAZING RITUAL

Eye-gazing is a wonderful practice for developing the heart connection and is used, for example, in Neo-Tantra and Karezza. This simple ritual may be short, but it is very powerful. This eye-gazing exercise, more involved and intense than the one on page 82, is an ideal way of marking the start of your time with your lover.

On entering the sacred space you have created (see pages 86–97), greet your partner in a way that honors the divinity within you both. "Namaste" is ideal—it is a widely used Sanskrit greeting that means "I honor you as an aspect of God," or "I honor you as an aspect of myself." In Neo-Tantric practice it is often voiced at the start of any partner-work. You may, however, prefer to develop your own form of greeting to honor your partner's divinity, something that has special meaning and associations for just the two of you.

Left A royal couple look deep into each other's eyes during lovemaking on the terrace. Rajput School, eighteenth century.

Sit opposite each other at a comfortable distance and look steadily into each other's eyes. Keep your gaze focused but relaxed, without straining—it's fine to blink when you need to.

Steady your mind as well as your gaze, stilling its background "chatter" and placing your entire focus on your lover's presence. Visualize your partner's eyes as the gateway to their soul and look deeply into them, tuning in to their divine essence and enhancing your awareness of the sacred connection between you. If you should feel your attention slipping, just draw yourself gently back into their gaze and into the present moment.

Truly see your beloved as the embodiment of the divine and freely express your feelings of heartfelt love through your own eyes. Synchronized breathing can help concentration and intensify the connection (see page 112).

End the session with a full-body embrace that acknowledges and celebrates your recognition of the divinity within yourselves and your partnership.

All our lives we've looked
into each other's faces.
That was the case today too.

How do we keep our love-secret?
We speak from brow to brow
and hear with our eyes.

RUMI

Erogenous Zones

An hundred years
should go to praise
Thine Eyes and on thy
Forehead gaze.
Two hundred to adore
each Breast
but thirty thousand to the rest.
An Age at least to every part,
And the last Age should
show your Heart.

ANDREW MARVELL, *TO HIS COY MISTRESS*

Erogenous zones are the parts of the body that are particularly sensitive to arousal. The sexual organs are the obvious examples, but in Tantric and Taoist thought the entire body is considered to be an erogenous zone, and the freeing of energy can result in a whole-body sensual experience.

Aside from the genitals, some erogenous zones are more obvious than others. A woman's breasts can be exceptionally sensitive to touch, and some women find they can reach orgasm simply by having their nipples caressed, licked, and sucked. Men's nipples can also be highly erotic and are too frequently ignored. The mouth is one of the most sensitive parts of the body, and is both an erogenous zone in itself, and one of the most effective and exciting means by which to pleasure another's erotic spots.

Finding an unexpectedly erogenous area in your partner can be fun and an arousing exercise. It may be the earlobes, the toes, or the back of the knee. The key is to explore and experiment, playfully stimulating different areas in different ways—stroking, scratching, kissing, sucking—until you find the spot and the touch that makes your partner shiver with pleasure and delight.

Rediscovering erogenous zones is particularly important for lovers in long-term relationships, where it is only too easy to fall into habitual or perfunctory patterns, such as concentrating exclusively on speedy sexual arousal through genital stimulation. Instead, learn to explore anew your partner's hotspots, and to experience the joy of heightened sensitivity spreading throughout your entire body, from toes to crown chakra.

ZONES FOR MEN

Face and neck, nape of neck

Shoulders, chest, nipples

Back, small of back

Hands, fingertips, and palms

Perineum, penis

Buttocks, anus

Soles of feet

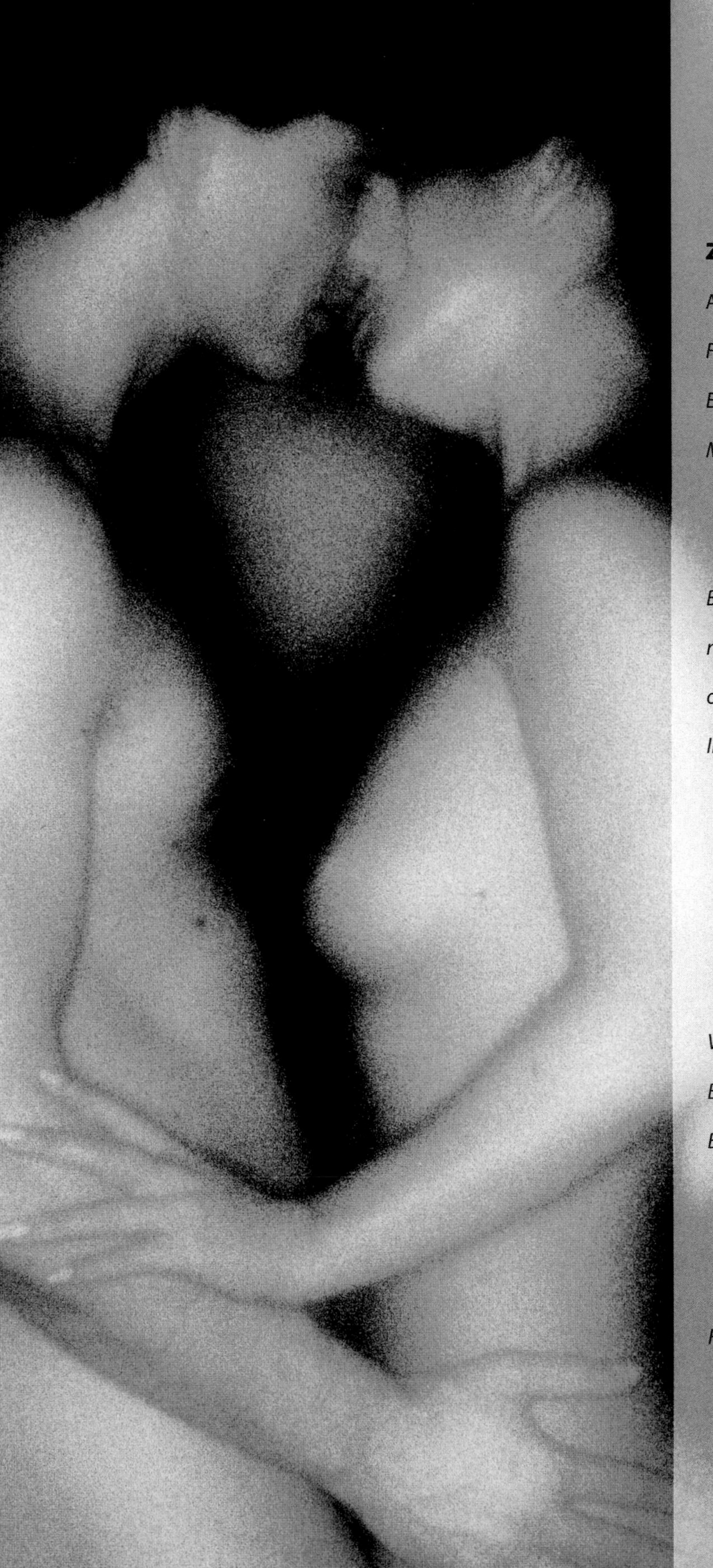

ZONES FOR WOMEN

All of the skin, but in particular:

Forehead, hairline, temples

Eyelids, eyebrows

Mouth, cheeks, ear lobes

Breasts, nipples, abdomen, navel, back of neck, back, base of spine, arms, armpits

Inside of elbow, hands

Vulva, clitoris, perineum

Buttocks, anus, inside of thighs

Back of knees

Feet

HEAD-TO-TOE WORSHIP

To seek to know every inch of your lover's skin fully is an incredibly intimate experience, and the understanding you gain deepens the sacred connection between you. The devotion with which you explore each other is an act of worship.

Set aside time to explore and map out your partner's body, inch-by-inch, from head to toe, awakening every erogenous zone and raising sexual energy throughout. You may well both end up in such a heightened state of arousal that further sexual activity follows, but this is not necessarily the aim. Try to keep your focus on touching, tasting, and smelling those parts of your lover's body you might not normally associate with a sexual response, and delight in the results.

Prepare your sacred space with suitable lighting, scent, music, and comfortable cushions. On entering it you may choose to inaugurate the sacred time with your "honoring the divine within" ritual.

Decide who will "give" and who will "receive" (this exercise works best if practiced consecutively rather than simultaneously). Set your imagination adrift and practice the art of tantalizing touch: hands can knead, press, and enfold as well as stroke, while fingertips can circle, trace, press, and scratch, so vary your touch and refresh the senses with change.

Intersperse feathery, teasing kisses with wide open caresses (especially around the breasts and buttocks). The *Kama Sutra* tells us that the parts of the body especially suitable for kissing are the forehead, eyes, cheeks, throat, breasts, lips, mouth, thighs, arms, navel, and penis, but all areas respond to the touch of soft lips.

Don't forget to use your feet and toes. Try running feet along calves and using toes to gently tweak or circle nipples—the contrast in skin texture is erotic for giver and receiver alike. Long hair can be used to stroke and trail across skin, or to trace the outline of lips, nipples, and navel. Have different sensuous materials on hand, such as feathers, silk, and velvet, for stroking and running along the skin.

Slow and continuous movement with a delicate touch is generally most pleasurable, and less is almost always more (especially when scratching). While listening to your imagination, intuition, and sense of spontaneity, you might want to pay particular attention to these areas:

Head: Gently hold your lover's head, allowing them to relax and surrender. Caress it slowly with your fingertips, stroking it and running your fingers through their hair.

Neck: Run your tongue from your partner's chin to the center of the collarbone, followed by licking and sucking the sides and lower jawbone (gently, to avoid disfiguring love bites), then softly bite and nuzzle the nape of the neck.

Ears: Nipping and sucking the ear lobes can be combined with caressing and massaging the tops of the ears.

Armpits: A very sensitive but commonly ignored erogenous zone, armpits contain the beginning of the heart channel and can be massaged gently with your fingertips or caressed with your tongue as a highly intimate and erotic act.

Nipples: Use the tip of your tongue to circle around the nipple; try a gliding and feathering stroke across the entire nipple, and experiment with combining sucking with very gentle biting.

Stomach: Try peppering soft, light kisses from the navel to the pubic area, or tracing an imaginary line between the two with your fingertip or tongue.

Base of Spine: Using your fingertips to apply light pressure to this area has a centering effect on the entire energy field.

Buttocks: These can take a firmer touch than other areas. They respond well to kneading, scratching, and gentle shaking, while the crease where each cheek meets the top of the thigh can be explored with your tongue.

Elbow Crease: Should be sucked as a prelude to running your tongue or blowing along the inner arm from elbow and wrist.

Hands and Fingers: Don't forget the creases between fingers, suck each knuckle in turn, and take time to blow small circles softly over each inner wrist.

Feet and Toes: Having lovingly washed your partner's feet beforehand as part of your *puja* or worship ritual, massage the sole of the foot gently, especially the point midway between the toes and the heel, the gateway to the soul in Taoist thought. Play with the toes, gently pulling and pressing each in turn, and using your tongue, if you wish, to explore the creases between the toes before sliding each toe, separately, into your mouth.

The sensitivity of different parts of the body may be governed by psychological factors, such as past experiences and associations, and the stimulation of particular areas can arouse strong feelings for a variety of different reasons. Some women find that massage of the stomach, in particular, produces feelings of tearfulness, so be prepared for any emotions that may emerge as you stroke and caress; be sensitive to your partner's responses, and pause and soothe if need be.

Sensual Massage

The awakening of erogenous zones can be turned into a full-blown sensual massage by learning the structured techniques of the basic massage strokes. These simple strokes, given with a loving touch, allow you to experience the joy of easing out tensions and stimulating your lover's entire body. Loving touch is one of the best forms of communication and, as you develop an erotic rhythm, you will be building up energy and releasing it throughout the body. As the massage-giver tunes into their partner, they combine different strokes to relax, penetrate, and tantalize, bringing every part of the body to life.

Preparing for a Massage

It is possible to buy ready-mixed massage oils, but making one up yourself can be fun and a sensual experience in itself. You will need a carrier or base oil, such as almond or grapeseed, to help your hands flow and glide over the skin, and essential oils to add fragrance. These should only ever be used in dilute form and never directly on the skin. Six drops of essential oil to twenty milliliters of base oil is a safe level, and makes a good quantity for a full body massage. Lavender oil works wonderfully as a relaxant, and for heightening sensual arousal you could add sandalwood and ylang ylang oils, which are considered to have an aphrodisiac effect, or jasmine and rose. Squeezy bottles for your prepared oil are useful: they are spill-proof and make it easy to judge the amount you are pouring out. Warm the oil by rubbing it between your hands before you start using it.

There are three basic massage strokes:

Effleurage: These are gliding strokes, used to spread the oil and make initial explorations of your beloved's body. This long, soothing touch, ideal for wide areas such as the back, usually begins the massage. The whole of the hand is used, in smooth movements, with even pressure applied. It is a gentle, relaxing touch. You can also circle your hands, with one on top of the other for greater depth.

Petrissage: This is a deeper technique, involving kneading and wringing, and is ideal for fleshy areas such as the buttocks. Push your thumbs in and away and use a squeezing, rolling, and lifting action. This stroke is great for loosening tense, knotted muscles.

Friction: For deeper work, thumbs or fingers can be applied with firm pressure, but be careful not to overdo it! Work along the direction of the muscle fibers rather than across them, and apply the pressure by leaning into the movement with the whole of your body rather than tensing your hands.

These are the basic strokes but, of course, there are many ways in which you can be creative in your sensual massage. Fingertip strokes, knuckles, heel of hand, squeezing, and percussion can all be put to good use, and there is no reason why you should limit yourself to your hands—try using your whole body, feet and toes, hair, even elbows. Try to keep some part of your body in physical contact with your lover at all times. The general direction of your strokes should always be toward the heart for blood flow.

Prepare a comfortable "mattress" of towels on the floor of your sacred space, making sure there is enough room for you to move around easily. Keep the lighting soft—candlelight is ideal—and play some gentle music. Most importantly, the space needs to be warm enough for goose-bump-free nakedness.

Don't forget to remove your watch and any jewelry, and to trim your fingernails if necessary. Massage can be surprisingly physically demanding, so stretch first to release any neck or shoulder tension and shake out your hands. While massaging, keep a good balance to allow yourself to move rhythmically, and avoid tensing your hands or arms. Do a deep breathing exercise with your partner beforehand and tune in to each other with eye-gazing (see pages 82–3) or forehead touching.

Your face shines with full moon splendor;
Your eyes, like lotus petals,
are exquisitely tapered.
Fragrant and white as a snowy conch shell,
You hold a glistening rosary of
immaculate pearls.
You are adorned by the beauteous
blush of dawn;
Like a lotus lake, your hands exude nectar.
Youthful one, white as an autumn cloud,
Many jewels cascade from your shoulders.
The palms of your hands are tender
and fresh as delicate leaves...
Your navel is soft as a lotus petal.

BHIKSUNI LAKSMI

A SENSUAL MASSAGE

This full sensual massage will take at least an hour. However, individual elements, such as the face or foot massage, can be enjoyed on their own if you have less time. The basic strokes can be put to good use at other times during your lovemaking too.

The first touch sets the tone for the whole massage and the back is a wonderful place to start. Glide up the back, along either side of the spine but not directly on it. Smooth up the center of the back, from pelvis to neck, one hand following the other. Stroke outward in a fan shape from the lower back and work upward.

Move down to the buttocks and, using effleurage strokes to spread some more oil into the skin, sweep your hands upward and outward. Circle with the heels of the hands, and knead (petrissage). The buttocks can take a firm pressure, so try knuckling as well.

Make long, smooth, sweeping strokes up the back of the legs, keeping a steady rhythm. Squeeze the calves and the thighs, also using the backs of your fingers to stroke up the thighs. Keep a steady rhythm—as one hand reaches the buttocks, start on the calf with the other. Take care with the sensitive back-of-knee area.

Ask your partner to turn over, and then use a tender, delicate touch on their neck as you kneel on either side of their head. Sweep your hands from the upper torso around the tops of the shoulders and along the back of the neck. Press slowly at the back of the neck to release tension. Roll the head gently from side to side, and then make small circles up the muscles on either side of the head. Knead the scalp, tousling and running your fingers through their hair.

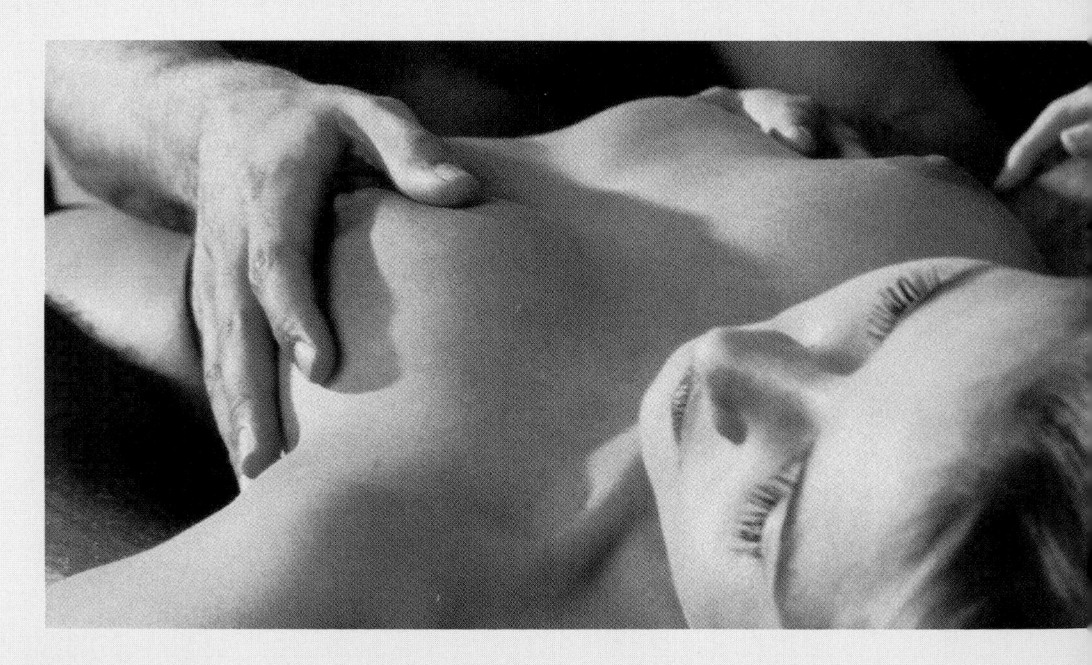

Gently massage the face with releasing outward strokes to ease the tension we habitually hold around the eyes and jaw. Place your thumbs in the center of your lover's forehead, then gradually and evenly draw them apart. Trace circles around the temples, smooth over the cheeks, and squeeze and pull the ear lobes lovingly. Encourage your partner to relax their jaw and mouth.

Move to the side and work on the arms, using effleurage and squeezing strokes. Work along the length of the muscles on the forearm, right up to the elbow. Use a similar squeezing action to work from the elbow to the shoulder.

Manipulate the wrists and massage the hands in turn, working around the joints with your thumb, giving each finger a light pull, and then softly caressing each palm with your fingers.

For the chest, use effleurage strokes to release tension and glide between and over the breasts or pectoral muscles. Take time to stroke, circle, and tweak the nipples.

Moving down to the abdomen, rest your hands lightly on the center of the stomach. This is a sensitive area for which gentle, warming contact with the flat of the hand works well. Try a circling motion, always moving in a clockwise direction, gradually allowing the pressure to increase.

Complete the flow of energy down the front of the body by moving on to the front of the legs. Work right up from the ankles to around the hips. You can massage quite deeply into the thighs, but ease the pressure as you reach the kneecaps—circling lightly to release pressure in the joint. Take care to work on either side of the shins when massaging the calves, as pressure on the bone can be quite painful.

Finally, give the feet some attention. Hold them softly and gently for a moment of stillness and grounding, then smooth over the tops of each foot with your thumbs, opening them out. Apply firm pressure around the toes, but be very delicate when you massage around the sensitive instep, unless your partner indicates they would welcome a firmer touch. Gently stretch and pull the toes, shaking them a little to help release tension. Pay special attention to the big toe—it is a *marma*, or power point, in Tantra and is said to be a replica of the entire body. After finishing with each foot, enfold it lovingly it in your hands for a few moments as your partner enjoys the sensation of relaxation.

End the massage with some uplifting, feathery strokes across the whole body, and then rest your hands lightly on your partner's body for a few moments to harmonize your energy.

Yoni Worship

Everything you can think of
Everything you can see,
Is a production of the Goddess.

JOSEPH CAMPBELL

Yoni (pronounced "yo-nee") is the Sanskrit word for the female sexual organs and means "sacred space." The cosmic yoni is the ancient sexual icon of the Great Goddess, worshiped in all early cultures as the source of life and sustenance. It appears in some of the earliest known art works: Cro-Magnon cave paintings from the Paleolithic period (c. 35,000–10,000 BCE) feature fertility symbols and Venus figures—naked female images with exaggerated sexual parts—and yoni goddesses appear in the mythology of every culture and era.

In Tantra, the yoni is worshiped as the gateway to direct experience of the divine, and *puja* rituals are performed to sculpted representations of the yoni, or to a partner's actual vulva. In addition to these explicit yoni icons, the lotus is often used to symbolize the yoni, represented in yantras and mandalas as a triangle, encircled by sixteen lotus petals.

Many women have ambivalent feelings about their sexual organs, and rarely take time to explore this sacred area visually or physically. Try using a mirror to really look at your yoni, to become familiar with its different textures, colors, and shapes. Think about the memories stored up there, and use your loving gaze and touch as an honoring and, if need be, healing process.

Yoni massage is a sacred and intimate act that deepens trust between lovers. The massage is done with a loving and nurturing, rather than intentionally stimulating, touch, with the aim of exploring and worshiping the goddess. It need not lead to orgasm, although this may well happen as a pleasurable side-effect.

PARTNERED YONI MASSAGE

The effects of this profoundly intimate massage can be overwhelming. If too much erotic energy starts to build, remind yourselves to relax, breathe, soften, and be present in the moment. Without the "goal" of orgasm you can relax into the experience and enjoy sharing a highly sensual worship ritual. A diagram locating the g-spot appears on page 177.

Prepare your warm sacred space, ensuring that everything that will be needed is on hand—have an oil- or water-based lubricant ready, set the music and lighting, and create a comfortable area with cushions. Prepare your bodies by bathing well (the massage-giver taking care to check and clip fingernails if necessary).

On entering the sacred space, focus your awareness with your "honoring the divine within" eye-gazing ritual. A shared breathing exercise will help you both to maintain awareness of your breath.

PARTNERED YONI MASSAGE (CONT)

The massage-receiver can lie on her back with pillows under head and hips, or lean back on cushions with the giver sitting cross-legged between her legs. Aim to be in a position that will be comfortable for a reasonably long period of time, one that allows the giver adequate "elbow-room" and enables you both to eye-gaze easily.

Throughout the massage the massage-giver should try to remain responsive so that the receiver does not feel she has to "direct." It can be very valuable to learn to surrender and let go of control, trusting your partner to explore intuitively. By maintaining eye-contact and through slight changes in body language it should be possible for the receiver to convey messages about the intensity of their feelings. Vocalizing emotions too much can draw you both away from the meditative nature of the exercise, but use words or noises to indicate if anything the giver is doing is causing pain or upset. There may also be moments when the receiver asks the giver to pause because the sensation has become too intense, she is nearing orgasm, or is simply feeling overwhelmed.

Maintaining deep, synchronized breathing, the giver begins by massaging the pelvic area, and the tops of the thighs, and the hips, looking at and appreciating the yoni, while awaiting an invitation to proceed further.

Once the invitation has been given, smooth oil over hand and fingers (warm the oil first in the palm of your hand), cup your hand over the mound and vaginal lips, re-establish eye-contact, then gently start to massage the mound and outer lips.

Circle a finger around the outside edge of the yoni, tracing along the outer and inner lips, and squeeze and stroke the outer and inner lips. Slide your finger up and down the length of each lip.

With your middle finger gliding along the outside of the yoni, use the two fingers either side to stroke the crease where the thigh meets the pubis.

Place the palm of one hand on her mound, resting your fingers lightly on the outer lips and your thumb on her opposite thigh. Lightly but firmly press your palm onto her mound and begin to move your hand in a tiny circular motion. Intersperse the circling with light taps on the vaginal lips. These are taps, not spanks, and shouldn't hurt. After giving the taps, rest your hand for a few seconds, then continue the cycle of circling and tapping. Approach the clitoris tenderly. Circle in a clockwise and an anti-clockwise direction, gently squeeze it between thumb and forefingers, and try light tickling.

Using more oil if need be, gently and slowly insert one finger into the vagina and hold completely still for some time while you both adjust to the sensation. Explore and massage the inner yoni, varying the depth, speed, and intensity. The thumb of the same hand can be used to stroke her clitoris at the same time. In addition to moving your finger, try slowly twisting your wrist.The g-spot or sacred spot, a slightly more ridged, spongy area of tissue just under the pubic bone and behind the clitoris, can be stroked and circled with the middle finger in a slightly curled position. This can be painful as well as pleasurable, and also arouse strong emotions, so be sensitive to your partner's responses. The yoni can also be massaged with lips and tongue, through kissing and licking.

While massaging the yoni, the giver's "free" hand can be used to glide over the rest of the receiver's body, caressing breasts, or massaging the stomach. This can build up erotic energy—to disperse it, use both hands to stroke away from the pelvis. The receiver may want to stroke her own body or stretch her arms out above her head.

Orgasm may occur once or a number of times as a result of yoni massage—and it is a good exercise in developing the ability to be multi-orgasmic—but the giver should continue until told to stop before very slowly removing their hands.

At the end of the yoni massage the receiver may want to be given some space to luxuriate in pleasurable feelings, but it can also be wonderful to "cocoon" yourselves together in a sheet or blanket and enjoy the glow of profound peace and contentment you will both be experiencing.

Can you hear me Mother,
sister, daughter, lover
Now that my heart is open
and I hold you in my eye
Now that I dream of Eagle
and my vision is as clear
as the mountain sky
Now that my breath
draws as deep as
my darkest dream
I can embrace the void that
separates us both,
You and I.

Now I can feel the serpent move
through this land
from the valley to the source
and back again
Now that I know the gentle wind
between the butterfly wing
I can reach out and touch you,
and hold you in awe
of the power in the thread
that life weaves
through us all.

ROB DREAMING, *TO THE WOMEN*

Lingam Worship

The erect phallus is the universal icon of male sexual power, and was often a feature in Paleolithic art. In Hinduism it is known as the *linga* or *lingam,* and it symbolizes the male energy of Shiva. Representations of the erect lingam can be found in temples and shrines throughout India, where it is worshiped as an emblem of fertility, generation, and recreation. Made of clay paste, wood, or stone, some examples have one or more faces of Shiva engraved or carved onto the side, or depict Shiva emerging out of a fiery lingam, linking the personified and iconic forms of the deity. Lingams may show a yoni at the base to represent the intertwining of the male and female principles and the inseparability of the two. Offerings of fresh flowers, fruit, pure water, and rice are made to the lingam as part of the worship ceremony. In Buddhist Tantra, the *vajra,* or thunderbolt, is a symbol of the erect phallus, and "the way of the *vajra*" is a special ritual of worship.

While traditionally it is an erect lingam that is worshiped, the softness of a real penis should be seen as part of its magic. It is, after all, soft more often than it is hard. The capacity to move from soft to hard and back again is a fantastic power that embodies the cycle of birth, growth, death, and rebirth that underlies our existence.

Lingam Massage

The lingam massage is a sensual exercise that helps men to learn to let go and surrender. Our society encourages men to focus on being "in control" sexually, to direct the action from a goal-oriented perspective. In this massage there is absolutely no question of pressure or performance. It simply invites you to lie back and be taken on a journey, surrendering to your partner's touch and resisting the urge to do anything or be anything. Although the focus is on your lingam, you may well feel warm waves of energy flowing over your entire body. In relaxing and trusting your beloved to worship your center of energy and sexual creativity, you are in turn worshiping their divinity too. So, just lie back and enjoy the experience.

For the massage-giver, the obvious pleasure of your lover, and the sense of his deepening trust as he lets go, make the act a highly intimate experience. Hold eye-gazing for as long as possible and be alert to any changes in body language, or sudden tension, so that you can anticipate any discomfort or concerns he might be feeling. You might want to establish verbal cues before you start so that he can let you know if he is nearing ejaculation, enabling you to slow down or stop before it becomes inevitable.

Preparing the Space for Massage

Prepare your sacred space for massage so that it is warm and comfortable. Use soft cushions and have a cover or blanket ready for when the massage is over. Use low lighting or candles, and set your music so that you won't have to stop the massage to change it. Scent the room with incense or essential oils. Make sure that massage oils and lubricant are on hand.

Both of you, having prepared your bodies by bathing and going to the bathroom (you don't want to have break the mood halfway through), should then enter your sacred space and perform your blessing ritual. This could be as simple as stating your intention for the sacred time ahead, and invoking a mood of tenderness, intimacy, and trust. Focus your awareness on each other using eye-gazing, and by synchronizing your breathing.

The Prostate

Men have a sacred spot that is equivalent to the woman's g-spot—the prostate. This is a small gland that is located within the pelvic bowl, between the lingam and the anus. The prostate becomes enlarged during sexual arousal. It contracts rhythmically during ejaculation, and releases a clear fluid.

PARTNERED LINGAM MASSAGE

The massage-receiver should be lying comfortably back on cushions, knees slightly bent and legs apart. The massage-giver can then kneel or sit cross-legged between his legs, in a position in which eye-contact can be maintained.

Take time to explore the lingam with your eyes, enjoying its shape and size while soft, the way it rests over the scrotum, and also the color and pattern of the hair covering the base and pubic bone.

Warm some massage oil in your hands, then gently smooth it over your partner's chest, sides, stomach, and thighs with sweeping massage strokes. Encourage your beloved to relax and breathe deeply as you ease the tensions from his body. Take as long as you need at this stage to set the mood with the gentle touch of your hands, reinforcing the idea that you have all the time in the world to play and love.

When the moment is right, pour some more oil into your hands and cradle the whole genital area while gazing deeply into his eyes. Gently begin to massage his scrotum, pubic bone, and perineum (the area between the scrotum and anus). Hold and caress his testicles, cupping them in your hand and supporting their weight. Gently pull and rub the skin of the scrotum, and stroke it lightly.

The lingam may or may not be erect at this point and it is not a matter for concern. The soft-hard cycle should be enjoyed for the magical process that it is, and some massage strokes are easier with a soft lingam.

Using more oil, start to massage the shaft of the lingam, working your way gradually to the head and back down again. Try just pulling up and sliding off a number of times, and then change direction so you are squeezing and sliding downward. Vary the speed and pressure you use and experiment with different types of massage strokes. Don't feel that you have to mimic the repetitive up-down movement of intercourse with your hands. Rather, try these variations:

Using plenty of oil, rub the lingam gently between both palms. Circle the head of the lingam with the well-oiled palm of one hand while wrapping the base of the lingam firmly with the index finger and thumb of the other.

As you slide up with one hand, start to slide up with your other before the lingam's head has emerged from the first stroke, and continue this action in a smooth rhythm, varying the speed from slow and gentle to fast and urgent.

Holding the base firmly so that the skin is pulled down, use your thumb and forefinger to "corkscrew" up and down the shaft. Find the most sensitive spot on the underside—usually just under the head—and gently squeeze, pinch, and nibble it.

When massaging the lingam with just one hand, be inventive with the other. Try cupping the testicles, tweaking nipples, massaging the inner thighs, or playing with the hair around the base of the lingam.

Occasionally remind your lover to focus on his breathing, particularly if he feels he is nearing ejaculation. In this case, slow down, change your stroke, or move your hands away from the lingam, allowing it to soften before continuing. As the erotic fire builds and subsides, you are practicing ejaculatory control, which leads to prolonged and multiple orgasms.

The prostate can be stimulated to great pleasurable effect from without and from within, and the lingam massage is an ideal time to explore this area as your lover is both aroused and relaxed. Externally, the point to press is located in the perineum, which is between the scrotum and anus. Try pressing in different places and with different intensities, and have your lover let you know when you have reached the "magic spot." Check the intensity with him—you may well find that you can press much harder than you initially think. This is the area to press firmly when on the brink of orgasm in order to delay ejaculation.

Internal stimulation of the prostate is a delicate and sensitive act. Direct contact with the prostate increases sexual arousal and satisfaction, and learning to relax the anus and buttocks almost always leads to greatly heightened sexual sensations. However, this is also a highly charged area about which many men have fears and tension. Gentleness and communication are vitally important when exploring this secret and vulnerable organ.

When you are stimulating the prostate internally, check, and keep checking, that your partner is comfortable, so he can be confident that there will be no sudden, painful movements, and you can remain confident that you are continuing to give him pleasure.

STIMULATING THE PROSTATE

It may be easier for the massage-receiver to lie on his front, but try and position yourselves so that he is lying on his back. This allows for eye contact, and enables the giver to support his lower back with one hand, which can provide reassurance.

For reasons of hygiene, it is advisable to wear a surgical latex glove, and it is essential that you use plenty of water-based lubricant. Exploring your lover's prostate is a very intimate exercise, involving high levels of trust, and should be performed with tenderness and love.

After gently massaging the rim of the anus, enter with the index or middle finger just a small distance—less than quarter of an inch—then stop. As you both get used to the new sensation, remind your partner to focus on his breathing. When he is ready to continue, try softly vibrating your finger to relax any tensions, then slowly move further

in. Stop again, breathe together, and let your partner talk about what he is experiencing. As you move deeper in, try moving your finger, massaging slowly and gently in circles. If you encounter areas of tension, press gently on the spot to ease it. Massage the perineum from inside, while supporting the base with your thumb outside.

Moving your finger deeply in the direction of the pubic bone, begin to feel for the prostate. It is a small round body of tissue nestling in the surrounding area (see page 177). Massage all around this sacred spot, vibrating your finger gently as your partner offers guidance on exactly where and how to apply pressure.

When he feels at ease he may want to self-pleasure his lingam, or have you do it. He may possibly experience whole-body waves of energy as his level of arousal mounts. He may also experience a deep emotional release, and feel the urge to laugh, cry, or scream. Encourage him in this, letting him know that you are there for him. During the exercise, take deep, full breaths and it can be helpful to maintain the energy charge with love muscle squeezes.

When the massage reaches its conclusion, ask before removing your finger, and do it slowly and in stages. Remove your gloves and wash your hands well.

Allow plenty of time afterward for talking, cuddling, and sharing. The bond between you will have been deepened by this experience, but you might both feel quite vulnerable, even shaky, after exploring this taboo area, and need time and space to integrate these new feelings. The anus can be a storehouse of repressed energies and all kinds of memories and emotions may be brought to the surface by opening it up. The massage giver should be prepared to listen, comfort if need be, and offer reassurance.

Foreplayfulness

The mystic dances in the sun,
hearing music others don't.

"Insanity," they say, those others.
If so, it's a very gentle,
nourishing sort.

RUMI

Of all the emotions that can be awakened, your sense of humor can provide the most long-term benefits for a happy and fulfilling sex life. Sacred sex is not a solemn experience but a joyful journey, a celebration of love and openness. Stopping from time to time to see the funny side of what you are doing is no bad thing. Being able to laugh together, especially at ourselves, is part of the process of letting go. It enables the barriers we have all learned to put up against the world to be broken down, and greater levels of trust and intimacy to develop; trust is the key to greater relaxation.

Collapsing into laughter as you encounter the apparent impossibility of some of the more complicated positions set out in the classic love manuals is perfectly normal, and is partly a recognition that you trust each other enough at least to attempt something new and challenging together, and that you feel comfortable about not succeeding every time.

Playfulness, and a childlike sense of awe and wonder at the incredible world around us, is a vital element in sensual spirituality, and nowhere more so than in lovemaking. Foreplay gives us the perfect opportunity to have fun together in ways that reawaken our inner, carefree spirit, allowing us to shed the worries of the day with laughter. Playfulness cannot be taught; however. It comes from within. Its spontaneity and light-heartedness reflect the

realization that the present is what matters, and these qualities are results of being able to live each moment to the fullest. All your powers of imagination and creativity come alive when you enter the special time of awakening sensual energy.

In the spirit of playfulness, here are some suggestions aimed at sparking off your own thoughts about what might be fun and pleasurable for you.

Explore the erotic potential of playfulness by "stripteasing" for your lover. Prepare a "stage" area in your sacred space, put on some suitable music, and perform a slow and seductive shedding of your clothes.

Try playing the game of finding your "inner wild animal," then acting it out for a set time. Lolloping and rolling around the room, roaring or growling your heads off, can be hilarious. It also performs a valuable "releasing" role as you begin to feel free to vocalize and let go of stresses and strains with animal noises.

Dance with, or for, your lover. Dancing can be energy raising (such as in Kundalini Shaking on pages 115–17) and highly sensual. Try mystic dancing—mirroring each other's natural movements and gestures to create harmony of mood. Express your desire and connection through dance—you could reflect orgasmic bliss in your movements, as in some forms of Middle Eastern belly dancing. Depict your relationship with the archetypal gods and goddesses by improvising sensual movements honoring the divine in your partner. You could also include eye-gazing and synchronized breathing to align your energies, and introduce touch. Lightly caress each other's face and hands, or touch meltingly with your whole bodies as you move together to the music.

Role play with each other. Play at being different people. When worshiping the divine within, take your visualization of each other as the archetypal cosmic couple a stage further by dressing up and decorating your faces and bodies with make-up and body-paint.

Blindfold your naked lover and touch them tantalizingly with different textures. Use feathers, silk scarves, or velvet cloths; roll smooth, round surfaces over their body, or massage devices.

The Inuit people to this day call sex "making laughter together," while Taoists cultivate the "inner smile," in the belief that when we smile our organs produce essences that nourish the whole body. Remember these happy words as you pursue the path of spiritualizing your sex life; sacred sex is not an earnest undertaking but a quickening of life and an awakening of sparkling joy.

CHAPTER 7

Channeling Energy During Lovemaking

In sacred sex, mental approach is far more important than technique. The highest delights are experienced through bringing awareness to our lovemaking. If you are spiritually prepared—through meditation, energy work, and heart-opening—and mentally attuned to your lover, and to the energy flows between you, any position can yield pleasure and touch something deeper.

However, there are ways in which energy can be channeled more effectively within and between our bodies by creating harmonious and stimulating circuits. Taoist delayed-ejaculation techniques and different thrusting methods can prolong and increase ecstasy.

Channeling energy during lovemaking is as much about non-doing as it is about doing. Relaxing and expanding into your love and passion, rather than contracting, allows sexual energy to flow smoothly between you, building up the erotic tension and intimacy.

In the Mood for Love

Male belongs to Yang.
Yang's uniqueness is
that he gets aroused quickly.
But he quickly retreats.
Female belongs to Yin.
Yin's uniqueness is that
she is slower to be aroused,
But she is also slow to retreat.

WU HSIEN

The ancient Taoist masters saw male and female sexuality in terms of Yin and Yang and compared them to fire and water. They likened male Yang energy to fire because it is easily ignited and doused. Yin energy, on the other hand, was like water because women are slower to bring to the boil and take longer to cool down.

The Taoists realized that without knowledge of how to harmonize these differences, sex was likely to be brief and, for the woman at least, deeply unsatisfactory. Men had to learn to arouse their lovers so that abundant energy could be built up before attempting penetrative intercourse. They were then taught how to delay their own orgasm, even to the point of avoiding ejaculation altogether. Instructional texts on the arousal levels of women often took the form of a dialog between a couple.

For example, one of the classic Taoist love texts is ascribed to the Plain Girl, who was one of the three sexual initiators of the Yellow Emperor. In *Secret Methods and Sexual Recipes of the Plain Girl*, she explains that, before sexual intercourse can take place, the body's energy system must be prepared for the intense stimulation to follow, and that lubrication of the Jade Gate (yoni) and the hardening of the Jade Stalk (lingam) are the first fundamental signs of the interplay of Yin and Yang.

The Plain Girl describes exactly how a man can discern whether his lover is sufficiently aroused for sex. He must pay attention to the responses and actions known as the Five Signs, the Five Desires, and the Ten Stages of Loving.

The Five Signs describe the involuntary sexual responses of an aroused woman. These are: a reddened face; hardened nipples, and beads of sweat around her nose; parched throat and dry lips; a wet and slippery Jade Gate; and, finally, a thick and viscous liquid running down her thigh. At each of these signs, she advises what action the man should take, from gentle stroking of the outer lips of the Jade Gate, to deep thrusting within.

The Five Desires relate to a woman's response to her lover's actions, and how, by watching out for these, he can adjust his technique to meet her desires. The first desire is intent, and is indicated by a quick pulse and shallow breathing during foreplay. The second desire is awareness, with flared nostrils and parted lips showing that she would like her Jade Gate stimulated. The third desire is the peak of passion and is reflected in the rhythmic movements of her body. The fourth desire—concentration—is reached at orgasm and is accompanied by a warm sweat. The fifth desire happens when her eyes close and her body straightens out and becomes rigid, indicating a state of heightened, ecstatic orgasm.

Finally, the Ten Stages of Loving describe the voluntary actions a woman takes to indicate to her lover what she would like him to do next. The first stage occurs when the woman embraces her lover fully and shows that she wants his Jade Stalk to draw close. The second stage is when she stretches out, arching up on her buttocks, indicating that she would like more attention paid to her Jade Gate. Thirdly, she will stretch her stomach and thighs, suggesting that penetration should commence. At the fourth stage, her "buttocks move about in joy," demonstrating deep pleasure. Desiring deeper thrusting is indicated by raising her legs and clasping her lover with her feet—the fifth stage. Sixthly, she will squeeze her thighs closely together, attempting to grip the Jade Stalk more firmly. At the seventh stage she moves her body rhythmically from side to side to indicate that she would like thrusting from left and right. Eighth, she will press her upper body and breasts against her beloved, a sign that she is nearing climax, followed by relaxing her entire body in the ninth stage as waves of pleasure roll across her. At the tenth stage her vital essences are released from her Jade Gate, showing that she is fully satisfied.

While these ancient teachings may seem somewhat formal and rigid to us today, there is an important general point within the archaic presentation—that sufficient foreplay and an understanding of each other's state of arousal is essential for truly transcendent sex. This requires us to allow time for attunement and for sexual energy to build up, entailing an increased awareness of each other's flow of energy and levels of arousal. The tuning-in together exercises before foreplay described on pages 82–3 can help you to become more sensitive to your partner's responses, and the head-to-toe worship (pages 132–3) and sensual massage (pages 136–7) are ideal for raising and spreading sexual energy throughout your bodies.

Prolonging Pleasure

The second of the main Taoist concerns was ejaculation control. The Taoists held that while women have an inexhaustible supply of Yin energy, men have a limited amount of Yang essence. If men ejaculate too frequently they are weakening their bodies and minds in the long term. Men were taught to absorb as much energy from their lover as possible, by bringing her to orgasm, while conserving their own energy through semen retention.

According to the Taoist masters, ejaculation should be limited by a man's age (young men can afford to ejaculate more often than older men) and according to the season (loss of essence should be avoided altogether in the cold of winter, but is permitted once every three days in spring, and twice a month in summer and autumn). Delaying ejaculation does not mean forgoing orgasm, because orgasm and ejaculation are physiologically distinct—ejaculation is

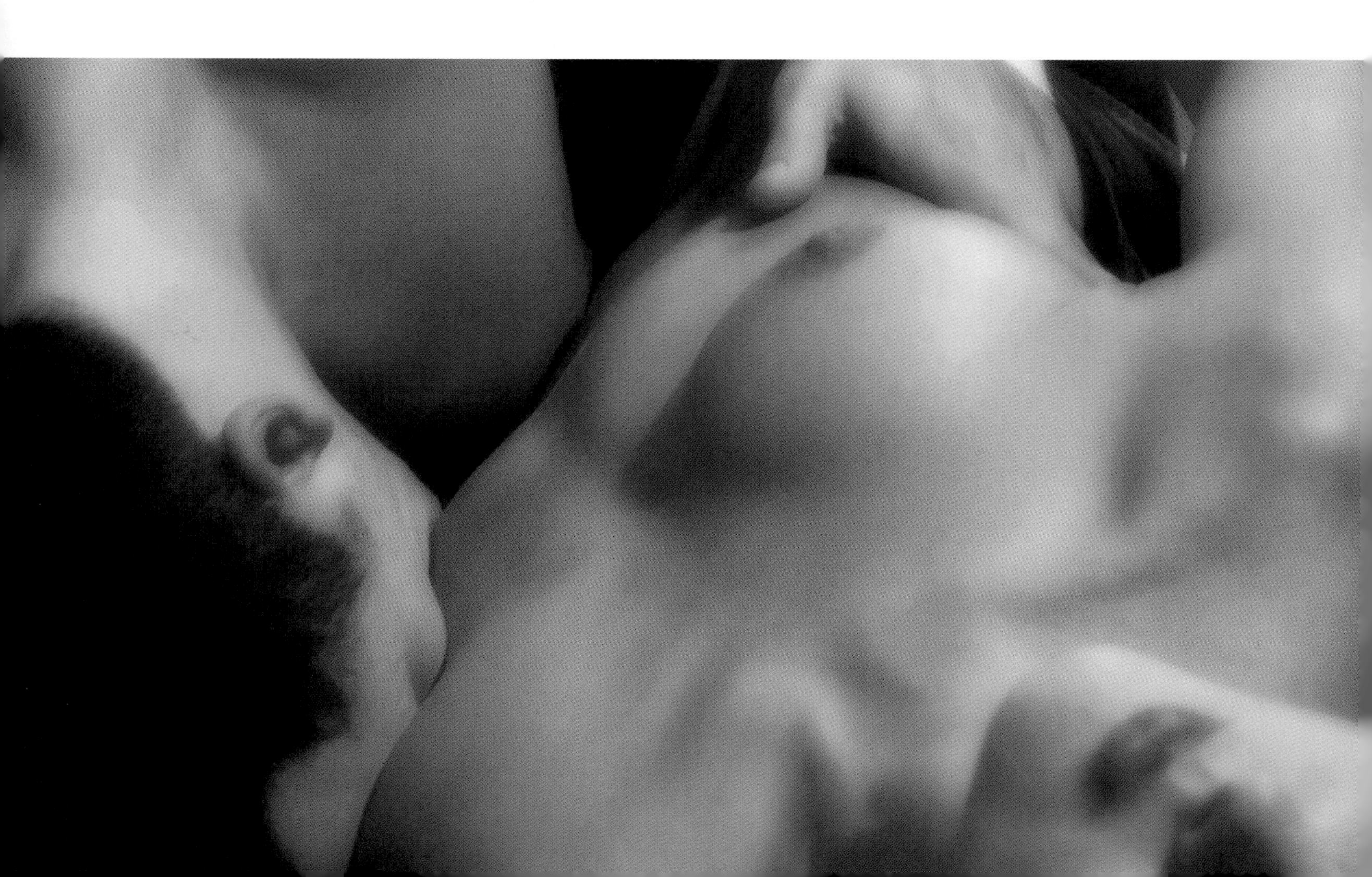

In sexual intercourse, semen must be regarded
as a most precious substance.
By saving it, a man protects his very life.
Whenever he does ejaculate,
the loss of semen must then be compensated
by absorbing the woman essence.

PENG-TZE, *SECRETS OF THE JADE BEDROOM*

an involuntary muscle spasm that generally, but not necessarily, accompanies the feeling of intense pleasure and release at the moment of orgasm. With practice it is possible to separate these two sensations. This involves learning to recognize when you are reaching the "point of no return," experiencing the pelvic contractions of orgasm, and then decreasing stimulation in order not to tip over the edge into ejaculation and detumescence.

Taoist thoughts on the importance of semen conservation for a long and healthy life may seem extreme. There is certainly a debate over the extent to which men really do become weaker through ejaculation, and the ethics of seeking to absorb a lover's essence while retaining one's own are doubtful. However, there are other, very good, short-term reasons for learning to delay ejaculation, even if you choose not to follow the path of total semen retention. Becoming aware of the difference between orgasm and ejaculation enables you to experience more intense climaxes and even multiple orgasms. Arousal is felt like a wave, a massive expansion of sexual energy that encompasses a series of peaks of sensation rather than one big climax. The longer you can make love, the more healing energy you can generate and circulate, and the greater the likelihood that you will be able to satisfy your lover more completely.

One cannot manage the myriad matters
Of Heaven and Earth,
Unless one stores up energy.
Storing energy means absorbing essence,
And absorbing essence doubles one's power.
Doubling one's power, one acquires a strength
That nothing can overcome.

TAO TE CHING

By experimenting with awareness of different levels of arousal and getting to know your "point of no return," you are getting to know your body and its sexual response better. This will free you to choose the type of lovemaking that feels right at a particular moment.

Taoist techniques for delaying ejaculation range from the fairly simple—the breathing, thrusting, and squeezing methods described below—to others that tend to be more esoteric and involved. The first of these, breath control, can be effective in slowing down arousal enough to avoid the "point of no return." Breathe slowly and deeply through the nose rather than the mouth to lower your heart rate. It can also be helpful to repeatedly hold the breath for a few seconds.

Deep, rhythmic breathing can also be combined with changes in your thrusting technique. If deep thrusting is creating too much excitement, try deliberately slowing down, matching your thrusts to your breathing, and switching to more shallow movements. Circling with the pelvis, rather than thrusting, can also help.

Pressing the tip or base of the lingam with your thumb and fingers can help, but can be awkward during lovemaking as it requires withdrawal. The perineum press is easier—just reach around and firmly press the area between the scrotum and the anus for a few seconds until arousal has subsided. An alternative is to "push out" with the love muscle. For a much more detailed explanation of Taoist beliefs on ejaculation control, and full exercises on how to develop this technique, Mantak and Maneewan Chia's *Taoist Secrets of Love* is highly recommended.

When first starting to explore the potential of delayed ejaculation, it is easier to experiment during self-pleasuring rather than when making love. This will give you a clearer idea of your personal sexual response, and of the sensation of reducing stimulation just before you reach the critical "point of no return."

When you do decide to introduce your newfound skill into your lovemaking, it is vital that you discuss it with your lover. Delayed ejaculation has clear benefits for many women, but without an understanding of the reasons for it, and of the physiological and psychological difference between orgasm and ejaculation, it may seem like a threatening development, with your lover feeling that she has "failed" to bring you to a climax.

If, after learning more about the principles behind the Taoist or Tantric view on semen retention, you decide to follow this path in a strict way, be aware of the danger of focusing on your own efforts, and on your own personal spiritual development, to the detriment of your sexual relationship in general. Generosity of spirit is a cornerstone of true sacred sex, and becoming obsessed with preserving semen at all times can result in a selfish, egocentric attitude to lovemaking. If your concentration is consistently on your own behavior rather than your lover's, you will fail to be in the moment, and the overall quality of your lovemaking will suffer.

It can also be counter-productive. Worrying too much during lovemaking about not ejaculating will lead, in turn, to anxiety and tension, which makes it more likely that you will ejaculate anyway. The key to ejaculation control is to relax and keep your mind in a calm state (the meditation techniques in Chapter Three will help) while remaining aware of your state of arousal, and then consciously to choose (or not choose) to apply your favored technique when the moment arises. If you try to delay ejaculation but leave it that little bit too late and pass the point of no return, just let go and enjoy it, rather than berate yourself for your perceived lack of success.

Kissing

The kiss is the gateway to bliss and amorous experience. The kiss provokes erotic ardor, agitates the heart, and is an incitation to the natural gift of self.

KAMA SUTRA

Deep erotic kissing creates a powerful energy circuit, but it is often neglected in long-term relationships. Think back to the hours you would spend kissing your first girlfriend or boyfriend, and recall the passion and intimacy this simple act of love could arouse.

Tantric and Taoist texts suggest a good reason for this. In Tantra the mouth is said to combine characteristics of both the yoni (the mouth and lips) and the lingam (the tongue). Mouth-to-mouth kissing is called "contact of the upper gates" and is capable of stimulating the chakras and conferring psychic protection.

In addition, Tantrics place particular value on a woman's upper lip, which is believed to be connected by a special nerve channel—called the "wisdom conch-like nerve"—directly to the clitoris. Opening up this channel can be achieved by kissing (try deep breathing and love muscle contractions while your partner nibbles and sucks on your top lip). Once awakened, it becomes yet another circuit for the flow of sexual energy.

Taoists also place a great emphasis on erotic kissing. There is an exchange of vital essences and energies in deep kissing, and saliva is believed to have properties that are effective in harmonizing the Yin and Yang forces in a couple. The essence produced by the "red lotus peak" (the lips) is called Jade Spring, and is first of the three Libations of the Three Peaks described by the ancient Taoist master Wu Hsien.

Be playful. If you are in a long-standing relationship in which deep kissing has been neglected, make an effort to reintroduce it. The next time you are about to give your lover a perfunctory peck on the lips, try exploring their lips and mouth more fully, and rediscover the joy of a long, sexy kiss. Lick and suck your partner's mouth, gently nip with your teeth. Use your fingers as well to play around the edges of the mouth, inserting them to be sucked. Kiss around the mouth, and the upper and lower lips in turn. Be delicate as you engage in a game of dancing tongues, retreating and advancing, darting and circling. Such kisses may lead on to something more, or simply be an intimate interlude in your daily lives, a helpful reminder of the passion you felt at the start of your relationship.

The *Kama Sutra* has the following suggestions for kissing which can be fun to explore:

The straight kiss: when the lips of both lovers are brought in direct contact with each other.

The bent kiss: when the heads of both lovers are bent toward each other.

The turned kiss: when one partner turns up the face of the other by holding their head and chin.

The pressed kiss: when the lower lip is pressed forcefully.

The greatly pressed lip: when the lower lip is held and touched with the tongue and pressed forcefully.

The kiss of the upper lip: when a man kisses the upper lip of the woman, while she kisses his lower lip.

The clasping kiss: when one of the partners takes both lips of the other between his or her own lips.

Fighting of the tongue: when one of the lovers touches the tongue, teeth, and palate of the other with the tongue.

Oral Erotic Energy Exchange

plum blossom close to the ground
her dark place opens
wet with the dew of her passion
wet with the lust of my tongue

IKKYU

Kissing need not only be mouth-to-mouth in order to confer the benefits of energy exchange. Kissing the breasts and nipples of a woman releases the second of Wu Hsien's Libations of the Three Peaks—White Snow. Kissing various energy centers of the body with conscious intent aids the flow of energy and confers psychic protection, as demonstrated in the *nyasa* exercise on page 121.

Kissing, sucking, and licking the yoni or lingam creates a powerful and stimulating energy circuit. Male lovers are especially advised in Tantric and Taoist texts to give oral pleasure to their partners as another way of worshiping the yoni, and the woman's sexual essences are seen as particularly potent—the third of Wu Hsien's Libations of the Three Peaks is the Moon Flower, created by the Jade Gate when a woman is excited. The Taoists called oral sex "tongue kung fu," and they developed exercises to strengthen the tongue and mouth so that this important part of lovemaking could be better performed. Simple exercises include sticking the tongue out fully for a minute or so, practicing curling up the edges of the tongue to form a roll, and stretching it out to the left and right.

The "69" position, or "the crow," in which stimulation is mutual as you lie head to toe, is used in Tantra to circulate sexual energy, and can be highly arousing. It forms a harmonious shape whether performed with the man on top, the woman or top, or in a sideways posture. However, oral stimulation need not be mutual for a circuit to be created, and some people find that in the "69" position it is difficult to enjoy fully the sensations they are receiving, or to focus on the pleasure they are giving their lover. If you feel the energy flow is being disrupted, then simply take it in turns—the energy circuit will still be active, and the "receiving" partner can also stimulate the "giver" manually from the same position.

Right Tantric lovers create a circular energy flow in this erotic temple carving at Khajuraho, Madhya Pradesh, India.

The *Kama Sutra* recommends an eightfold path to "mouth-congress" when a man is being orally pleasured:

Nominal congress: the lingam is softly and gently caressed by the woman's mouth.

Biting the sides: the lingam is nibbled while being held.

Outside pressing: the head of the lingam is gently sucked.

Inside pressing: the whole of the lingam is given long, deep sucks with the whole of the mouth.

Kissing: the lingam is kissed all over.

Tonguing: the lingam is licked all over.

Sucking the mango fruit: the lingam is sucked fiercely with about half of it in the mouth.

Swallowing up: deep sucking of the whole of the lingam.

Body Yantras

And when is it that man is called one? When man and woman are joined together sexually. Come and see!
At the point at which a human being as male and female is united, taking care that his thoughts are holy, he is perfect and stainless and is called one. Man should therefore act so that woman is glad at that moment and has one single wish together with him, and both of them united should bring their mind to that thing.

ZOHAR

The adoption of different postures during lovemaking allows the subtle energies to converge and exchange. The harmonious shapes we create with our bodies to channel energy are like yantras, the mystical centering diagrams used in meditation, discussed on page 73. These body yantras help in the conscious circulation of energy by aligning chakras and connecting energy centers.

With a little thought about the placing of your bodies and limbs, it is easily possible to increase the energy flow between you by matching up parts of your body to create simple circuits. Try mouth to mouth, forehead to forehead, palm to palm, or back to back for harmonizing energy. Even the most basic posture—the classic missionary position, with the man lying on top of the woman—allows for a great deal of energy flow as a number of similar body parts are touching: you can look into each other's eyes easily to maintain your soul-gazing connection with each other, and can complete the circuit through the mouth and tongue with deep, erotic kissing.

The yab-yum posture—which represents the union of male and female principles and cosmic oneness in Tantra—also allows similar parts of the body to meet, as the woman sits in the man's lap with her legs and arms wrapped around him. This is a very peaceful position, enabling you both to visualize the flow of energy moving upward, through and around your bodies while eye-gazing and kissing. A limited amount of friction can be achieved in this intimate position by gentle rocking of the pelvis. If you are breathing synchronously, try rocking slightly forward as you inhale and backward as you exhale. You can help circulate the energy by using your hands to stroke along the spine. Yab-yum also allows for still passion, as all the action can occur internally through the squeezing and relaxing of the love muscle.

In these postures you can incorporate the shared and complementary breathing techniques described on page 112, and visualize the sexual energy moving around the circuit created by your bodies. One way to do this is to lie face-to-face comfortably and connect an energy center, such as the heart chakra, or third eye if you touch foreheads. Inhaling, visualize energy coming into that center from your partner. Then, exhaling, visualize energy flowing out into your partner's energy center from yours.

Left Tibetan Buddhist bronze statue of Vajrasattva, the Supreme Buddha, embracing Visvatara, the Supreme Wisdom, in the yab-yum position.

Match dissimilar parts of your bodies for stimulating energy, as in the "69" position. Rear-entry postures are also effective at generating this kind of energy, and allow for manual stimulation of the clitoris and deep penetration.

Consider the positions of your hands and feet—in Tantric thought they are microcosms of the body and may be used to make contact with the interior of the body. When joined, they can channel energy that may otherwise flow outward and be lost. A wonderful position in which to experience this circuit is with the woman lying on her back between the legs of her seated partner. Each can hold the other's feet while sharing a breath connection and eye contact. A more advanced position—the "totally auspicious posture"—offers a variation on this circuit. While united, the man can lift his lover's feet up to his head and, holding them with both hands, touch the soles to his ears, nose, mouth, and crown.

Another classic Tantric posture is the Kamachakra (wheel of kama). In the Kamachakra the couple's legs and arms form the spokes of a wheel: starting off in the yab-yum position, but then both stretching out and parting their legs. Hands can be placed on each other's shoulders as you lean backward, or joined with arms extended out sideways to create an even more harmonious yantra.

The "woman on top" is a Tantric posture that gives the woman control over the depth of penetration, pace, and the flow of energy. She can visualize pulling her lover's energy upward through her root chakra, along her spine, and then flowing it back to him down her arms and through her palms into whichever part of his body she is touching. She can also imagine it moving back down her spine and returning to him through the root chakra.

Try exploring different circuits and feel how the energy between you shifts and flows as you make contact with different parts of your body. If you find that the energy seems somehow to be getting "stuck," the solution may simply be to change position. If, however, you find yourselves getting overheated, then a peaceful posture, such as yab-yum, in which you can cool down while still remaining united, is ideal. Experiment and discover which postures offer the most stimulation—Tantric texts recommend that lovemaking should always begin in positions that offer the woman the most pleasure, as it generally takes her longer to become aroused. It can also be exciting to move between different postures as a kind of erotic dance, staying genitally and energetically connected, and keeping as much contact between your bodies as possible as you flow from one body yantra to another.

Rhythms of Love

Above Lovers in the "Wheelbarrow" position. Chinese print from the series illustrating the lives of the Mongols. Tao-kuang period, c. 1850.

Taoist love texts place great emphasis on thrusting—style, rhythms, and number. One reason for this is simply that Taoist love sessions can last a very long time, and it was thought that varying the type and depth of the thrusts could prevent tedium from developing. Another reason is that different thrusts, at different speeds, intensities, and depths increase the nuances of pleasure for both man and woman, and also aid men in controlling ejaculation.

In the seventh-century Taoist text *T'ung Hsuan Tzu*, nine types of thrust, all of which can be employed with great effect today, are described in characteristically poetic language:

1) Strike out to the left and right, as a brave warrior trying to break up the enemy ranks.
2) Move up and down, as a wild horse bucking through a stream.
3) Pull out and push in, as a group of seagulls playing on the waves.
4) Use deep thrusts and shallow teasing strokes, alternating swiftly as a sparrow picking the leftovers of rice in a mortar.
5) Make deep and shallow thrusts in steady succession, as a huge stone sinking into the sea.

6) Push in slowly, as a snake entering a hole to hibernate.
7) Thrust swiftly, as a frightened rat rushes into a hole.
8) Poise, then strike like an eagle catching an elusive hare.
9) Rise and then plunge low like a huge sailing boat braving the gale.

"Nine shallow, one deep" is one of the thrusting rhythms recommended by the Taoist masters. This varies the level of stimulation for both partners, and helps the man to control ejaculation. The deep thrust creates a vacuum by pushing air out of the yoni, a sensation intensified by the following shallow thrusts that do not break the "seal" of the vacuum, but hover in the first inch or two of the yoni, and stimulate the g-spot.

Different shallow/deep rhythms also work well, but the Taoists prefer to stay with odd numbers (these are regarded as more auspicious)—so try five shallow, one deep, or seven shallow, one deep. Or you could work up in sequence by trying nine shallow, one deep, followed by eight shallow, two deep, seven shallow, three deep, and so on, until you reach one shallow, nine deep.

Deep thrusts in which the lingam is drawn fully along the length of the yoni can sometimes be too stimulating for the man to curb. Some may find it easier to control arousal levels with short, deep thrusts, in which the lingam stays deep within the yoni and is thrust forward and drawn back only a short distance. This rhythm has the added advantage of stimulating the woman's clitoris through the close contact with her lover's pubic bone.

"In and out" action is just one rhythm of love, of course. There are many possible variations. Hip circling can be highly arousing as it stimulates all the walls of the yoni and is also good for sending energy up the spine.

Rhythms of love need not only be created by the male partner's thrusting. Squeezing and relaxing the love muscle is a crucial way for the woman to get sexual energy flowing through the body, and it helps increase arousal levels.

When the "nine shallow, one deep" technique is being used, try giving a brief squeeze as the lingam is being withdrawn during the shallow thrust, and a longer squeeze that lasts the duration of the deep thrust. Another pleasurable technique is to squeeze slowly as your partner slowly enters or withdraws. With shallow entry it can be exciting to tighten the entrance of the yoni by rhythmically contracting the muscle around the head of the lingam.

Love-muscle contractions also allow you to focus on the energy produced by this powerful rhythm, and visualize its passage around the body, while you remain motionless.

Peaceful Pauses

In a rhythm, as any drummer will tell you, the space between the action is as important as the action itself. Amid all the thrusting, the principle of "non-doing" should not be forgotten, and pausing while united is a wonderful way to experience peaceful intimacy. It is a time to take a breath, re-establish your gaze with your lover, get a calm and powerful sense of the energy moving between you and, perhaps, enjoy sudden insights. Pausing can also help to prolong your sexual union by cooling your ardor and thus delaying the climax.

After allowing plenty of sexual energy to build up, try taking a pause during the throes of passionate lovemaking. Both of you should simply stop completely for a minute or so, and feel your heightened energy and sensations continue to rush while you experience peace and oneness. The yab-yum position is especially suited to peaceful pausing as you can easily look into each other's eyes, and appreciate the closeness of your intertwined bodies.

Neither movement from nor towards,
Neither ascent nor decline
Except for the point, the still point,
There would be no dance,
and there is only the dance.

T.S. ELIOT, "BURNT NORTON," *FOUR QUARTETS*

Imsak

Imsak is an ancient Arabic sexual method that combines pauses with specific thrusting rhythms to create the fullest accumulation of energy and arousal. It relies on the man being able to delay ejaculation (*imsak* means "retention"), and this is facilitated in Imsak by the frequent pauses, which here involve complete withdrawal. If practiced in full this is a fairly long and involved technique, but one which repays the time and effort spent with such an accumulation of erotic tension and energy that the final release is spectacularly satisfying.

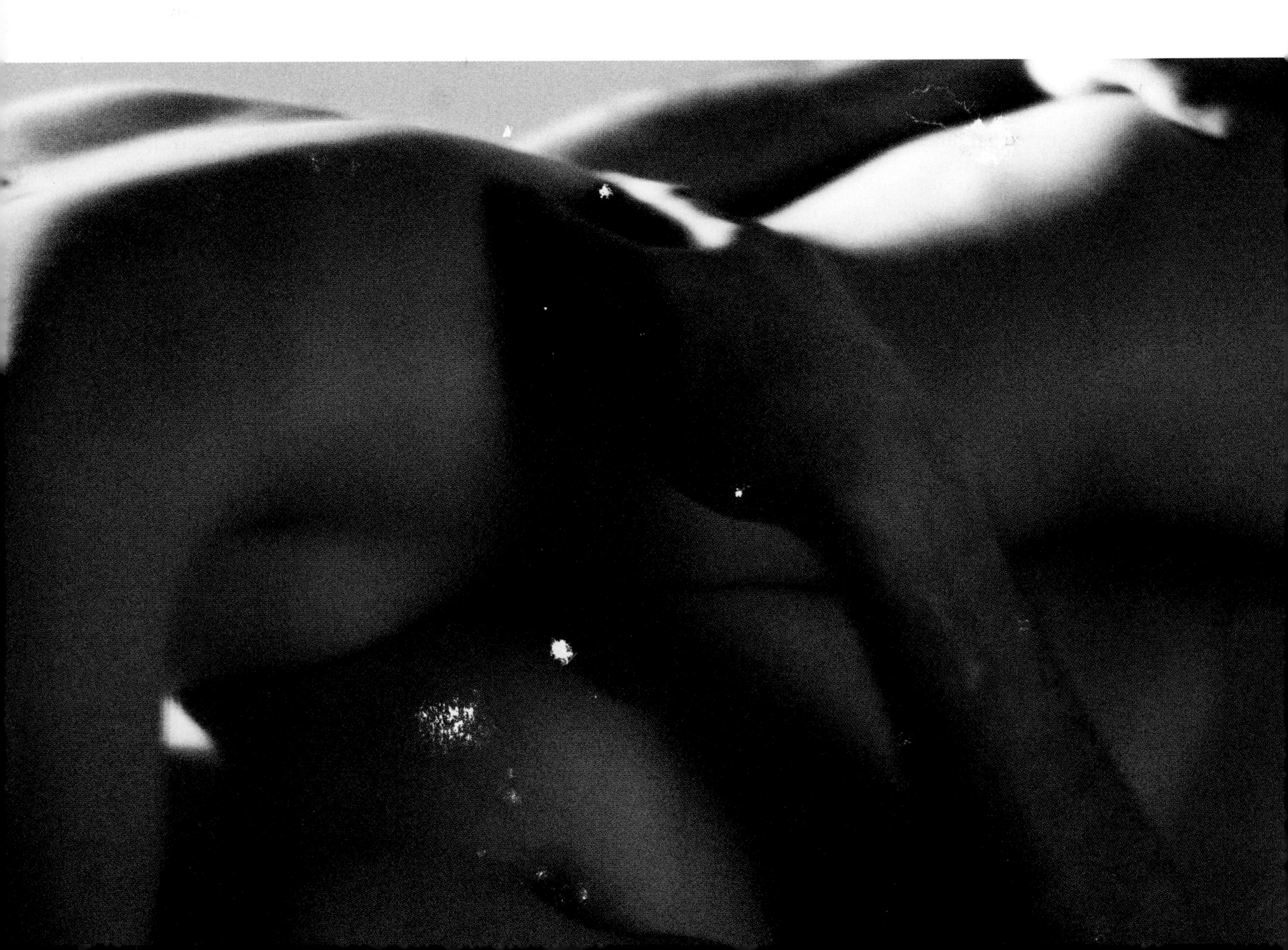

With the woman on top, a series of ten cycles is performed. The first five do not involve much movement. The man enters fully but does not thrust. To maintain arousal both partners should work their love muscles so that all the action occurs internally. The woman can also stimulate her clitoris with her fingers in this position. When arousal reaches such a peak that ejaculation is near, the man should pull out for a cooling-off pause. Once the danger period has passed and his erection has subsided, the pause can be filled with affectionate stroking, kissing, eye-gazing, or meditation together. Eventually arousal starts to heighten once more and it is time for re-entry.

After five cycles of motionless union followed by breaks, the stage is set for some thrusting. The technique is to thrust ten times before pulling out. The first three are shallow thrusts, followed by two fast, deep thrusts. Three more shallow thrusts follow, then two slow, but very deep.

Once more, take a pause until desire wanes and rises again, then have one more love muscle cycle, a pause, another thrusting cycle, a pause, and yet another motionless union. Having reached the tenth and thrusting cycle, the man is ready for an intense voluntary climax. The woman may have already reached orgasm, or have held back for a final, mutually transcendent tidal wave of bliss.

Imsak may seem to be quite a stilted form of sacred sex, and it is probably not the best technique to suggest to a new partner. However, for lovers who are used to each other's responses it can be turned into a flowing sexual dance as you move in and out of union with each other and use the space in between to enjoy a profound sense of intimacy. These periods of stillness are also ideal for practicing the non-penetrative, energy-exchanging methods suggested on pages 120–1, remaining energetically connected while not reaching "dangerous" levels of arousal.

Elements of Imsak can also be incorporated into lovemaking without engaging in the full cycle (although it is worth doing at least once, just to experience the intense pleasure produced by prolonged erotic tension). Try two motionless cycles with breaks, followed by thrusting, before moving on to a different position.

You know what happens when we touch!
You laugh like the sun coming up laughs
at a star that disappears into it.

Love opens my chest, and thought
returns to its confines.

RUMI

Karezza

If no attempt is made to induce orgasm by bodily motion, the interpenetration of the sexual centers becomes a channel of the most vivid psychic interchange. While neither partner is working to make anything happen, both surrender themselves completely to whatever the process itself might feel like doing.

ALAN WATTS, *NATURE, MAN AND WOMAN*

The technique known as Karezza takes "non-doing" to its ultimate conclusion. Based on the Italian word for "caress," the term was coined by a pioneering nineteenth-century obstetrician, Alice Bunker Stockham. One of the first women to qualify as a doctor in the United States, and a radical advocate of women's and children's rights, Stockham fitted sacred sexuality into a Christian paradigm (although her technique could be used by couples of any or no religious persuasion), and promoted sexual equality within spiritual sex. She used the metaphor of a fountain slowly filling a basin, drop by drop, to describe the accumulation of sexual energy. The build-up of sexual desire continues day by day until the basin naturally and gently overflows. If the basin were drained dry through repeated orgasmic activity before it was filled naturally, then the drained person would be in a state of energy depletion. This applied to both men and women, and so Stockham's teachings ran counter to traditional Hindu Tantric techniques. She viewed these as unfairly allowing women to "drain their basin" by having orgasms, while men were taught to exercise restraint in order to preserve their vital essences and to benefit from the orgasmic sexual energy of their female partners.

Stockham believed that sexual union should be planned in advance—she recommended that couples have separate bedrooms so that meeting for sex would be intentional—and that it should be preceded by some form of spiritual dedication, such as lighting candles, writing love letters, or reading poetry (she particularly liked Ralph Waldo Emerson and Elizabeth Barrett Browning). Religious affirmations or prayers could also be said during intercourse. Sexual union lasted for an hour, and involved no bodily movement at all. The purpose of this practice was to increase the feeling of loving unity with each other, rather than the retention of energy for its own sake. She believed that orgasm would occur naturally when the "basin" overflowed (but that this would not necessarily happen in every sexual encounter).

During Karezza the lovers may gaze into each other's eyes for a prolonged period and breathe a "love-saturated breath" together, sharing their deep feelings of love and affection for each other. The mood is relaxed and contemplative as both seek to lose their individual natures in cosmic consciousness. It may be necessary to move occasionally in order to maintain arousal, but this ideally is achieved through contracting and relaxing the love muscle so that the motion is internal and does not distract the mind from its deep, meditational state.

Stockham's Karezza may seem rather formal, but it is ideal for couples in an established relationship who want to explore the depths of their intimacy. She also believed that it gave rise to a transcendent state of consciousness:

> *At the appointed time, without fatigue of body or unrest of mind, accompany generally bodily contact with expressions of endearment and affection, followed by the complete quiet union of the sexual organs. During a lengthy period of perfect control, the whole being of each other is merged into the other, and an exquisite exaltation experienced. This may be accompanied by a quiet motion, entirely under subordination of the will, so that the thrill of passion for either may not go beyond a pleasurable exchange. Unless procreation is desired, let the final propagative orgasm be entirely avoided. With abundant time and mutual reciprocity the interchange becomes satisfactory and complete without expression or crises. In the course of an hour the physical tension subsides, the spiritual exaltation increases, and not uncommonly visions of a transcendent life are seen and consciousness of new powers experienced.*

Afterplay

The importance of afterplay—prolonging the mood you have created—is often ignored, but it can be as vital as foreplay. Sacred sex doesn't end when you reach orgasm. Moments of profound intimacy and spiritual illumination occur while you are still energetically connected and breathing together. This is also a time of mutual absorption of essences, and of the further exchange of energy.

Take time getting out of position and move into a comfortable "resting" posture (such as side-by-side). Try to avoid the temptation to roll over and go to sleep, or to let your mind start jumping ahead to all the things you have to do with the rest of the day. Instead, allow yourself to bathe in the afterglow of your loving union, feeling the waves of tingling post-orgasmic energy rippling through and between you. With your heart connection fully opened, this is a special time together. Be gentle with each other. You have both opened up totally to one other—physically, emotionally, and spiritually—and you may just want to lie closely and quietly together in the moment.

As you slowly begin to gather your thoughts, this can be a good time to talk openly and honestly, and share feelings, sensations, and emotions. It could be a time for affirmation, for telling your lover how much you liked it when they did this or that, and how it made you feel.

You may be feeling a bit spaced-out or light-headed after your sacred sex experience. This is perfectly normal. After all, you have been raising powerful energy within yourself and with your lover. Do some grounding exercises, such as those set out on pages 122–3, to restore your balance. Taking a bath or shower together or sharing food is also grounding, and enables you to continue to enjoy this intimate time while you prepare for your re-emergence into the busy world outside.

This slow time is also important in terms of integrating the powerful feelings or insights you might have experienced during your sacred union. It may be hard to verbalize what you are feeling at this stage, and you may find yourself worrying that the experience is already slipping through your fingers like sand. Don't try to grasp it to stop it disappearing—by "coming down" gently you are allowing time for the experience to sink in and be given a place and meaning, making it possible later on to make sense of it within the context of your everyday life.

Of course, lying intertwined, stroking, nuzzling, and cuddling, talking over the sensations you have just shared, may eventually lead you to want to start the experience all over again—afterplay merging into foreplay in one delicious circle of pleasure.

And Beyond...

A road might end
at a single house,
but it s not love s road

Love is a river.
Drink from it.

RUMI

The afterglow of sacred sex extends beyond your time of union, and even beyond your post-coital cup of tea, shower, and gentle re-emergence into the world.

During your lovemaking you may have reached heightened states of consciousness and gained insights into the divine mystery itself. However, after the physical sensations have gone, the sweat has dried, and the bed been remade, these insights can fade to no more than a remembered glimpse of something greater, unless they are brought back from that special place and time and integrated into your everyday life.

The Buddhist teacher Jack Kornfield said, "after the ecstasy, the laundry." This is as true for the ecstasy of spiritual sex as it is for any other kind of peak experience. In sacred sex the sexual act is the vehicle—a highly pleasurable vehicle—that brings us to a different level of awareness, in which we reconnect with our own spiritual essence, and so with the interconnectedness of all things. This awakening and integration of body, mind, heart, and spirit does not confine itself to the bedroom. Re-affirming the place of spirit in our life is a joyous and celebratory transformation that profoundly affects all our relationships, whether sexual or not. The spiritual connection that is experienced through sexual intimacy continues after the lovemaking itself is over and acts as a beacon of light on the world, suggesting new possibilities, and new ways of interacting with and relating to the people around us.

Sacred sex is about saying "yes" to life—to *all* of life. By bringing awareness into the expression of our sexuality, we can grow and extend that expanded consciousness into all aspects of our lives. Having awakened our senses through intimacy with each other, we can carry that sense of openness, of embracing, to every encounter, every obstacle, every joy that we encounter. We come to realize that by being fully alive in the present, we find new opportunities for celebrating a more sensual form of spirituality around us everywhere.

In honoring our own sexual energy, and recognizing and respecting it in others, we are tapping into the greatest creative force. With that awareness, our sexuality becomes not something to be suppressed and locked away until we are in bed with a lover, nor an appetite that enslaves us with its demands, but a gift to be cherished.

There is a school of Zen Buddhism that is known as the Red Thread Path. It teaches us that our bodies are the lotus of the true law, inextricably linked to the eternal cycle of birth and death through the red thread of passion. The joyful and expansive path of sacred sex affirms our place within this infinite thread of passion that runs through all of life.

Appendix I: Anatomy of the Love Muscle

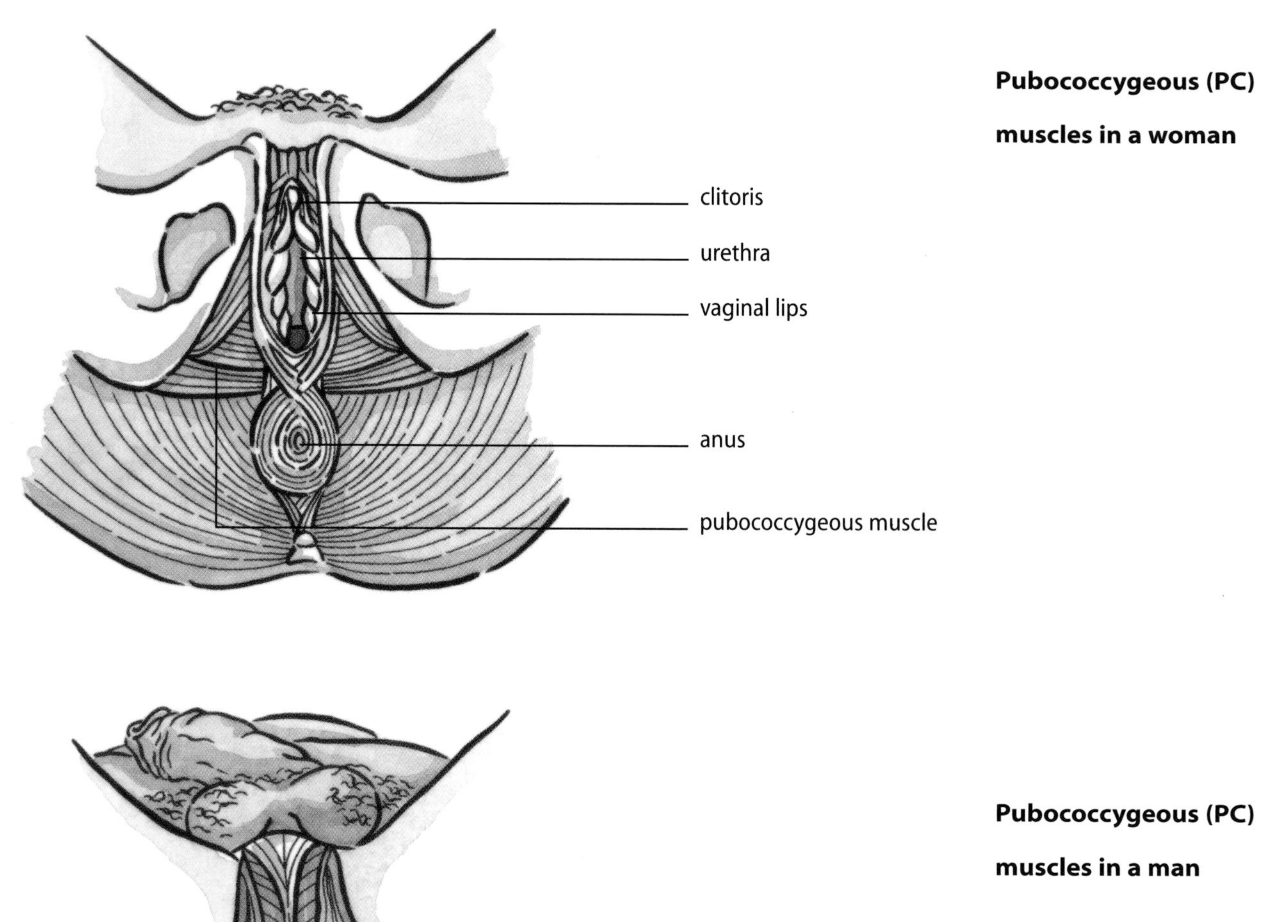

Pubococcygeous (PC) muscles in a woman

perineal muscles
anus
pubococcygeous muscle

Pubococcygeous (PC) muscles in a man

Appendix II: Internal Massage

Stimulating the g-spot

The g-spot in women is a small pleasure point in the upper part of the vaginal channel. When stimulated, it swells and grows firm and can lead to an orgasm in which a clear fluid is released. This "female ejaculation" is described in Tantric texts.

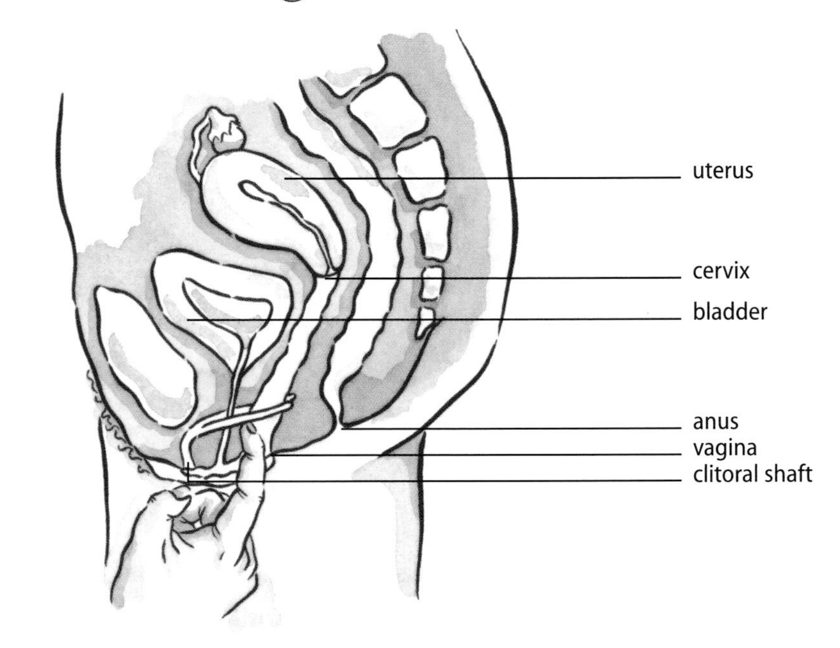

Stimulating the prostate

The male equivalent to the g-spot is the prostate, a small gland located in the pelvic bowl between the lingam and the anus. This swells during sexual arousal, and contracts and relaxes rhythmically during ejaculation, producing a clear fluid.

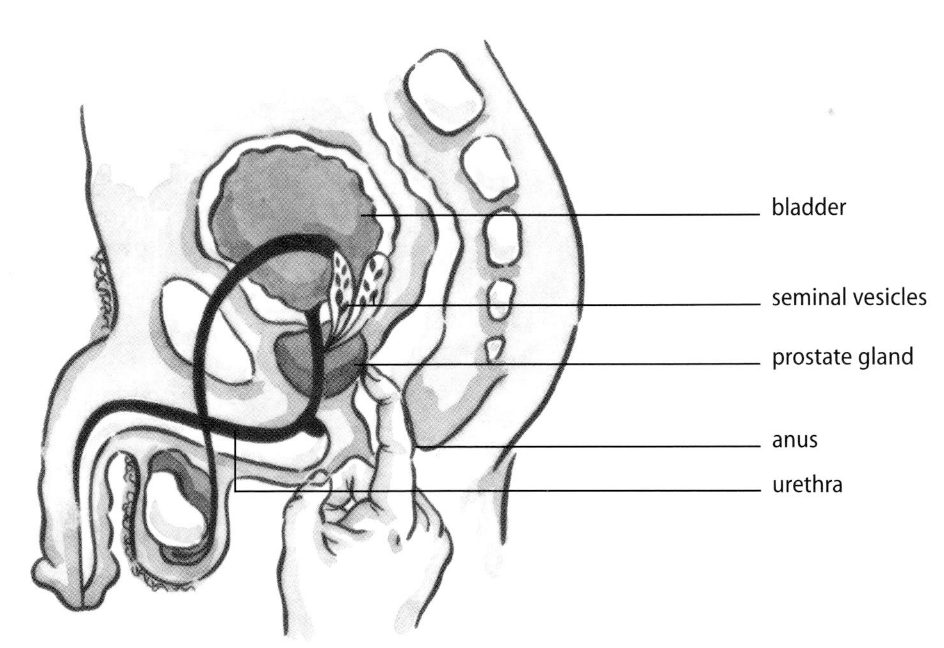

Glossary

Ajna "Command from above." The chakra located at the third eye.

Anahata "Without sound." The heart chakra.

Bindu An energy point, usually shown as a dot in the center of a yantra to represent the source of supreme energy.

Chakra "Circle" or "wheel" in Sanskrit. Chakras are vortices in the subtle body that represent a concentration of conscious energy.

Chi For Taoists, the life force, primordial energy.

Ching In Taoism, our fundamental sexual energy.

Great Rite Sacred ceremony within the Wiccan tradition, representing the spiritual marriage of goddess and god.

Kabbalah The mystical tradition within Judaism.

Koan Paradoxical statement, or "riddle," used to aid meditation in Zen Buddhism.

Kundalini The powerful, latent female energy within us all. Located at the base of the spine, it is represented by a coiled snake. Also referred to as Shakti-Kundalini.

Lingam Penis or phallus, either actual or symbolic, that represents Shiva energy when erect.

Love muscle The pubococcygeous (pelvic floor) muscle that can be developed to increase pleasure.

Magickal Childe An effect on the astral plane, created during intercourse in Sex Magick rituals.

Maithuna Ritual sexual intercourse in which a couple make love as the divine goddess and god, Shakti and Shiva.

Mandala Circular drawing used in meditation. It can also mean a sacred space or refer to the yoni.

Manipura "To shine like a jewel." Third chakra, located in the solar plexus.

Mantra A sacred sound in the form of a syllable or phrase, used as a meditation aid to align ourselves with the divine.

Meditation The practice of stilling the mind, often through focusing on an object such as a yantra or a sacred sound (mantra).

Mudra Ritual hand gesture used in devotional and meditation practice. Also refers to the roasted beans used in the central Tantric ritual.

Muladhara "Root support." The first chakra, located at the base of the spine.

Namaste Greeting used in Hindu society to express "I honor you as an aspect of the divine."

Neo-Tantra Adaptation of traditional Hindu and Buddhist Tantra taught in the West.

Om The supreme mantra, it represents the original sound of the Creator and the spontaneous vibrational sound of the universe. May also be written as AUM.

Pranayama Hindu science of breathing.

Puja Devotion, ritual, and worship.

Sahasrara "Thousand-spoked." The crown chakra.

Shakti The Supreme Goddess and female energy of the universe embodied by all women, and depicted as a variety of different goddesses.

Shen In Taoism, our highest level of awareness, spirit.

Shiva The male energy of consciousness, and divine consort of Shakti.

Sigil A mystical, graphical representation of a magickal goal used in Sex Magick.

Subtle body The non-physical, pure energy body that animates and permeates our physical body.

Sushumna The central energy channel in the subtle body that connects the chakras.

Svadisthana "Abode of the self." Second chakra, located in the pelvis.

Sutra A spiritual text.

Tan T'ien Taoist energy field, located in the pelvic area, the solar plexus, and the head.

Tao Te Ching The short foundational text of Taoism, which appeared around the fourth century BCE and is attributed to the sage Lao Tz'u.

Three Treasures Sexual essence (*ching*), energy (*chi*), and spirit (*shen*) in Taoist thought.

Visshuda "Purified." The throat chakra.

Yab-Yum Sexual posture that represents cosmic oneness and the union of the male and female principles.

Yang The cosmic male principle in Taoism, represented by man, fire, and heaven.

Yantra Mystical, geometric drawing used as tool in meditation.

Yin The cosmic female principle in Taoism, represented by woman, water, and earth.

Yoni Vulva, either actual or symbolic, that represents Shakti energy. Can also mean "sacred space."

Above left and above Indian carved ivory panels showing Tantric love scenes.

Select Bibliography

Tantra

Aldred, Caroline. *Divine Sex.* London: Carroll & Brown, 2000.
An accessible, fully illustrated introduction to Neo-Tantric and Taoist sexual teaching.

Anand, Margo. *The Art of Sexual Ecstasy.* Los Angeles, CA: Tarcher, Putnam, 1989.
Anand, Margo. *The Art of Sexual Magic.* London: Piatkus, 1995.
Two classic best sellers from the leading teacher of Neo-Tantra in the West. These detailed manuals are based on Anand's SkyDancing training.

Douglas, Nik. *Spiritual Sex.* New York, NY: Pocket Books, 1997.
A detailed look at the origins of Tantra and its relevance to the twenty-first century.

Douglas, Nik, and Penny Slinger. *Sexual Secrets: The Alchemy of Ecstasy.* Rochester, Vermont: Destiny Books, 1979, 2000.
Wonderfully informative and beautifully illustrated book about traditional Tantra and Taoism that is let down by one extremely homophobic chapter.

Lorius, Cassandra. *Tantric Sex: Making Love Last.* London: Thorsons, 1999.
Based on Margo Anand's SkyDancing Neo-Tantra, this is a good introduction to the subject that doesn't neglect to mention traditional Tantra's cultural origins.

Shaw, Miranda. *Passionate Enlightenment: Women in Tantric Buddhism.* Princeton, New Jersey: Princeton, 1994.
A fascinating work that presents new evidence of the outspoken and independent female founders of Tantra. Academic in style, but highly readable.

Taoism

"Barefoot Doctor" (Stephen Russell). *Barefoot Doctor's Handbook for Modern Lovers.* London: Piatkus, 2000.
Irreverent guide to "truly rude and amazing love and sex" from a "wayward Taoist."

Chang, Jolan. *The Tao of Love and Sex.* Aldershot, Hampshire: Wildwood, 1997.
Interesting overview of Taoist techniques.

Chia, Mantak and Maneewan. *Taoist Secrets of Love: Cultivating Male Sexual Energy.* Santa Fe, NM: Aurora Press, 1984.
Chia, Mantak and Maneewan. *Healing Love through the Tao: Cultivating Female Sexual Energy.* Santa Fe, NM: Healing Tao Books, 1986.
Chia, Mantak and Maneewan, Carlton Abrams, Rachel and Abrams, Douglas. *Multi-Orgasmic Couple.* London: Thorsons, 2000.
These three books set out the Chia's Healing Love system, based on Taoist sexual wisdom. All are thorough and practical guides (especially for the background, beliefs, and techniques of Taoist ejaculation control in the "male" volume), although the third is the more immediately accessible.

Reid, Daniel. *The Tao of Health, Sex and Longevity.* London: Simon & Schuster, 1989.
Sex is just one element in this rigorous look at the Taoist health sciences. Good for putting the sexual practices into context, and getting a sense of the bigger picture, but not a quick read.

Paganism and Sex Magick

Ashcroft-Nowicki, Dolores. *The Tree of Ecstasy: An Advanced Manual of Sexual Magick.* Leicestershire: Thoth Publications, 1991.
Complete set of rituals based on Sex Magick for those with a good grounding in the subject. Refreshingly direct author.

Johnston, Bonnie L., and Peter L. Schuerman. *Sex, Magick and Spirit.* St Paul, MN: Llewellyn, 1998.
Considers Sex Magick from the perspective of its Western cultural roots, looking at archetypes and myth. Contains good practical exercises and has an interestingly different outlook.

Kraig, Donald Michael. *Modern Sex Magick.* St Paul, MN: Llewellyn, 1998.
Excellent introduction to the subject that includes articles by women sex magicians. In contrast to many books in this field, this one is frank, open, and accessible.

Starhawk. *The Spiral Dance.* San Francisco, CA: HarperCollins, 1979.
Classic text from a famous Wicca practitioner and teacher. Good on sacred space and ritual.

Other

Fox, Matthew. *Sins of the Spirit, Blessings of the Flesh.* Goldenbridge, Dublin: Gateway, 1999.
Profound attempt to create an enlightened theology that challenges the traditional Christian view that "flesh" equals "sin." From the author credited with reviving Creation-centered Spirituality.

Mumford, Susan. *The Sensual Touch: A Lover's Guide to Massage.* London: Reed, 1994.
Beautifully photographed complete guide to giving a full sensual massage.

Ramsdale, David and Ellen. *Sexual Energy Ecstasy.* New York, NY: Bantam, 1985.
Fantastic, very practical guide to the sexual secrets of the East and West. The authors impart their comprehensive knowledge with a light touch and a playful sense of humor. Highly recommended.

Sudo, Philip Toshio. *Zen Sex.* San Francisco, CA: HarperCollins, 2000.
Poetic and inspiring work exploring Zen monk Ikkyu's "red thread of passion."

Left Erotic miniature painting from Jaipur, Rajasthan, India.

Index

Figures in italics refer to captions.

Acknowledgments

Grateful acknowledgment is made to the following, from whom I have quoted in this book. Page 6: *The Diary of Anaïs Nin,* Vol. 4 (New York: Harcourt Brace Jovanovich, 1971). Pages 12 and 135: Miranda Shaw, *Passionate Enlightenment: Women in Tantric Buddhism* (Princeton, New Jersey: Princeton, 1994). Pages 18 and 155: Daniel Reid (translation by R.H. van Gulik), *The Tao of Health, Sex and Longevity* (London: Simon and Schuster, 1989). Pages 39, 67, 72, 102, 158: Nik Douglas and Penny Slinger, *Sexual Secrets: The Alchemy of Ecstasy* (Rochester, Vermont: Destiny Books, 1979, 2000). Page 83: Margo Anand, *The Art of Sexual Magic* (London: Piatkus, 1995). Page 160: John Stevens (translator and editor), *Wild Ways: Zen Poems of Ikkyu* (Boston: Shambhala Publications Inc, 1995). Page 152: Mantak and Maneewan Chia and Douglas and Rachel Carlton Abrams, *Multi-Orgasmic Couple* (London: Thorsons, 2000). Page 93: Malidoma Patrice Some, *Ritual* (Gateway, 1996). Page 113: Alan Watts, *Nature, Man and Woman* (New York: Vintage, 1991). Excerpts from Rumi taken from: *Birdsong : Fifty-Three Short Poems, Jelaluddin Rumi,* Coleman Barks (translator) (Florence, AL: Maypop, 1993). Every effort has been made to trace all present copyright holders of the quotes used in this book. Any omission is unintentional and we will be pleased to hear from copyright holders and correct errors in future editions.

Picture Credits

p.1 Antonio Mo/Getty Images; p.7 © Larry Williams/Corbis Stock Market; p.13 Jean-Louis Nou/AKG London; p.17 The Bridgeman Art Library; p.19 Penny Brown; p.22/23 Jan Brueghel and Rubens, P. P./Mauritishuis, The Hague/The Bridgeman Art Library; p.26/27 Christine Osborne Pictures; p.29 Frieda Harris/Warburg Institute, London/The Bridgeman Art Library; p.33 Ranald Mackechnie/Stone; p.35 Trinette Reed/Stone; p.36/37 © Michael Keller/Corbis Stock Market; p.42/43 Werner Forman Archive, Private Collection; p.44 Anthony Marsland/Stone; p.50/51 © Claudia Kunin/Corbis; p.55 Antonio Mo/Getty Images; p.56 Penny Brown; p.61 Tony Anderson/Telegraph Colour Library; p.68/69 Victoria & Albert Museum/The Bridgeman Art Library; p.72 Penny Brown; p.74 Andy Weber Studios; p.75 Penny Brown; p.77 Austin Osmon Spare/The Bridgeman Art Library; p.78 Penny Brown; p.84/85 © C/B Productions/Corbis Stock Market; p.90/91 AKG London; p.95 Hywell Jones/IT Stock International; p.96/97 © Nation Wong/Corbis; p.98/99 Steven Still/IT Stock International; p.102/103 The Bridgeman Art Library; p.116 Trinette Reed/Corbis; p.127 Chris Stowers/Panos Pictures; p.128 The Bridgeman Art Library; p.131 John Knill/IT Stock International; p.139 Stefan April/Stone; p.159 Thomas Schweizer/Corbis Stock Market; p.161 Martyn Evans/Travel Ink; p.163 Werner Forman Archive, Philip Goldman Collection, London; p.165 The Bridgeman Art Library; p.176/177 Penny Brown; p.179 (above): Werner Forman Archive, Private Collection; (below): Werner Forman Archive, Private Collection; p.181: Roderick Johnson/Panos Pictures. Every effort has been made to trace all present copyright holders of the pictures used in this book. Any omission is unintentional and we will be pleased to hear from copyright holders and correct errors in future editions.